# Careful What You Wish For

# Careful What You Wish For

A Novel

By:

JESSIE ALLEN

authorHOUSE®

*AuthorHouse™ LLC*
*1663 Liberty Drive*
*Bloomington, IN 47403*
*www.authorhouse.com*
*Phone: 1-800-839-8640*



*Published by AuthorHouse 08/16/2013*

*ISBN: 978-1-4918-1083-5 (sc)*
*ISBN: 978-1-4918-1203-7 (e)*

*Library of Congress Control Number: 2013915016*



*This book is printed on acid-free paper.*

# Dedications

This book is dedicated to everyone who was willing to take a chance on me.

Thank-you

Also, to my husband Ken, for his continuous support and encouragement of fulfilling one of my dreams. I already filled one the day I met you.

And, for the two other dreams that became a reality and call me, Mom. You two make life very entertaining, and I'm very blessed to call you my son's. Love you guys.

***In loving memory of.***

***Little Roger Lee~1948-2013***

Knowledge speaks, but wisdom listens.

—Jimi Hendrix

# Epilogue

"Can I please see my daughter?," Haley pleaded with the uniformed officer through a strangled sob as her curled finger brushed against her runny nose.

"I'm sorry ma'am." Officer Davis replied remorsefully. "I just have a few more questions."

"Can't this wait until after I see her?" Haley's broken voice rose an octave through her outrage as she threw her hands up in the air, gesturing her annoyance. All she wanted to do was see Megan, but this infuriating man wouldn't allow that to happen. Grief and despair began to tear at her heart.

After arriving home from work, ironically enough she worked at the very hospital she now stood in, to a scene that no parent should ever bear witness to. Every time she closed her eyes, she relived the horrific images of red and blue flashing lights cutting into the eerie still night as her daughter's lifeless body was transported on a gurney to the awaiting ambulance. It all seemed surreal. Like any minute now she was going to wake up and realize it was just a bad dream.

There could be no way her happy, healthy, little girl could be laying in a hospital bed, fighting for her life. It just wasn't—

"I'm afraid not Ma'am." He cleared his throat as the tip of his thumb rubbed his clean shaven chin. "How long has Janice Welliver worked for you Ms. Martinez?" Officer Davis asked, proving she wasn't dreaming.

Haley's eyes searched aimlessly around the floor of crowded waiting room in the Emergency Room, trying to remember as she slowly ran her hands back and forth her folded arms, trying to ebb away the dismay.

"About two months?" There was an edge uncertainty to her voice. Her mind was clouded over with worry. Janice was the last person on her mind.

Wait a minute? A brief clearing of hazy anxiety cleared her grief stricken mind only to be replaced with an instant squeezing of fright in her chest. Why would he want to know about Janice?

"What does this have to do with Janice?" The somber expression that washed over Officer Davis's face created a nauseating sinking of despair in the pit of her stomach.

Oh God! She placed a shaky finger against her trembling lips as she spoke. "Is she the reason my baby's here?" Her tear strained whisper was barely audible. Waves for fear began to assault her, causing her body to quiver, as shaky hands flew up to cover the sob that threatened to erupt, her eyes filling anew.

Officer Davis briefly closed his eyes, as if it pained him to respond before he solemnly nodded his head. A sensation of intense sickness and desolation swept over her as a cold hand of anguish wrapped around her throat, making it difficult to breath.

"Ma'am. Is there anybody I can call for you?" She felt his warm hand grab onto her shoulder and heard the concern in his voice, but she wouldn't wrap her mind around what he was saying. A stab of guilt lay buried in her chest. This was all her fault. If she hadn't picked up those extra hours, Megan wouldn't be here.

"Megan Martinez?" The sound of the doctor's voice created a flash of wild grief to ripple through her. She whirled her attention in the direction of the voice. Her quick, jerky movements took her off-balance. Officer Davis placed a steady hand on her shoulder and guided her over to one of the waiting room chairs and helped ease her into it, preparing her for what the doctor was about to tell her. Officer Davis motioned for the older woman to come over.

"Ms. Martinez, I'm Dr. Williams." She began in a sincere doctor tone as she sat next to Haley and placed a concerned hand on Haley's knee. She gave a heavy sigh before continuing. "You're daughter is in fair, but critical condition due to the second-degree burns she sustained." Haley covered her face with trembling hands and gave vent to the agony of her grief.

Bitter cold despair dwelt in the caves of her worried soul a few hours later as she looked over her little girl's angelic body. If it hadn't been for the clear tubing of the IV taped to Megan's small hand, or the white gauze covering from her collar bone down to her belly, Haley would've thought nothing happened to her daughter.

Apparently, Janice decided to get drunk and pass out while she was entrusted to look after Megan's safety and welling being. That's what Officer Davis informed her of when he found her unconscious, surrounded by numerous empty beer bottles. Megan had watched Haley numerous times in the past, cooking in the kitchen and decided to feed herself when she became hungry and couldn't wake Janice, at least that's what the police were speculating at this time, since they found an overturned pan of cooked macaroni laying on the floor around Megan along with upturned kitchen chair. If it hadn't been for Cliff, her neighbor from across the street hearing Megan's anguished screams . . . a cold shuddered of raw awareness rippled along her spine as she mentally shook away those horrid thoughts. She was a woman facing the harsh realities of yet another letdown by someone she trusted.

This was an awakening experience that left her reeling. She knew Megan and herself were never going to experience that level of hell that they endured that night again. Nothing would ever make them feel that way again. Nothing.

September 2008

# Chapter 1

"Megan can take up to four of these pills a day, but no more than that." Dr. Warren the plastic surgeon, cautioned Haley as he handed her the prescription. Haley looked over it before placing on top of Megan's discharge papers.

"Make sure she gets plenty of rest. No activity that's going to stretch the skin graft, and keep the bandages dry on both the grafts and the donor site at all times." Haley nodded her head as Dr. Warren went over the rest of the at home care instructions.

"So kiddo?" Dr. Warren grabbed Megan's purple socked foot and gave it a playful shake, making her giggle. "I'll see you in a week to remove your bandage, and put another one.

Does that sound good?" Dr. Warren looked down at Megan's smiling face. Her smile was contagious as he too smiled wide.

"Can I have a Barbie band-aid this time?" Her voice was filled with excitement as she looked up at him expectantly, smiling from ear to ear.

Hearing Megan's precious little giggle, made the backs of Haley's eyes sting as a cold shiver swept over her, as she remembered the painful memories of that horrific night. She was so grateful to hear that wonderful sound. Something that she felt like she took for granted sometimes.

Megan had spent the past three weeks in the hospital recovering from her burns and the wave of infection that threatened her life. She had developed a staph infection due to her burns. The doctors quickly began treatment. When Megan's body broke out into hives, they were forced to seek another form of medicine, as she had an allergic reaction to the current choice. When they found one that would work for her, the infection had already entered into her blood stream, making her blood pressure plummet. She almost lost her daughter that night. She felt ice spreading through her stomach as she recalled the unpleasant memories.

Dr. Warren looked out of the corner of his eye, like he was deeply pondering her request, as his lips twisted, making Megan giggle again.

"I don't think we have any of them, but I'm pretty certain we have pink." Megan gasped as her eyes widened. "Mommy! Did you hear that?" She slowly craned her head towards Haley, being careful of the tanned, wrinkled bandage that clung to her neck, like a second skin. "They have my favorite color." She exclaimed.

Haley felt a pang of remorse as she watched Megan gentle movements. She swallowed past the lump that was forming in her throat. "That's great sweetie." Her best friend, Tanya demanded that she stop beating herself up. Preaching that it wasn't her fault Megan got burned. That was easier said than done. She couldn't shake the guilt that this was all her wrong doing.

Just as Haley packed away the rest of Megan's "get well" things, a knocking on the open door drew her attention to the door way. "There's my favorite girl." Haley didn't miss the mock delight in his tone. Megan's eyes darted nervously from the man that stood at the end of her bed, then over to Haley. She looked terrified looking up at the strange man. Haley took that moment to move over to her bed and brush her brown hair from her forehead as she placed a kiss where she just removed her chestnut hair.

"Mommy?" Megan's eyes searched the man's before she slowly turned her head towards Haley. "Who is that man." A low angry grumble sounded shortly after Megan spoke, startling her as she eyebrows drew together, and the sound of her crying filled Haley's ears. Haley quickly lifted her head and gave Adam a warning glare and then jutted her chin her towards the door.

"What? I'm not supposed to be upset that my own daughter doesn't even know me?" His harsh whisper was filled with outrage as they stood just outside of Megan's room.

Haley cocked her hip to the side as she folded her arms across her chest. "And whose fault is *that*?" She icily retorted, raising an eyebrow, challenging him.

He whipped his head towards Megan and turned back to face her. "Don't you dare put all the blame on me." He sneered as he stabbed an accusing finger towards her. His face twisting with anger.

Her stunned mouth dropped open as she stared at him in disbelief. Seriously? He was trying to put the blame on her? For something he did.

"How is she suppose to know you when you've never seen her a day in her life?" Her accusing voice stabbing the air as she permitted herself a withering stare.

He solemnly hung his head, and let out a heavy sigh, before his eyes reached hers again. "Look. I want to get to know my daughter." His tone was relatively civil despite his anger.

"Marry me?" He suddenly blurted out.

What? "What?!" She exclaimed in irritation as her face contorted into bewilderment.

"Marry me. That way I can get to know *my* daughter." His response held a note of impatience, but it felt like it was more of a demand then a question. She hesitated, blinking in bafflement.

A shadow of annoyance crossed his face when she said, with easy defiance, "No!" His lips puckered in frustration as his straight glance seemed to be accusing her coldly. "You're going to regret this." He harshly whispered. He backed away from her without haste, but with unhurried purpose. She tossed her head and eyed him with cold triumph.

After Adam left, she expelled the breath she hadn't realize she'd been holding.

Marry Him? Was he nuts?

There was more ways of getting to know his daughter, than being married to him. A smile curved her mouth as she absently shook away his ridiculous notion, but her smile soon faded as her mind searched anxiously for the meaning behind his words. Her stomach clutched tightly, and it was impossible to steady her erratic pulse.

Regret what? Sounds for the hallway suddenly startled her. She began to shake as fearful images built in her mind. Would he harm her? Would he harm Megan? Familiar panic she recognize from before, settled in her throat from the agonized unknown at the doing of Adam Lucas.

# Chapter 2

"Which pattern do you like, dear?" Judith Lucas inquired in a snobbish tone as she extended her over-jeweled arms in front of her to marvel the china clutched in her stubby fingers. Haley inwardly groaning as she suppressed the urge to roll her eyes. Judith, was Haley's soon-to-be monster-in-law from hell. That's right-Monster. The word mother represented someone loving and nurturing. That was so not Judith Lucas.

No! She was cold and insensitive, well just like a . . . monster. Haley didn't respond to Judith at first as she stared in speechless disbelief as the older woman turned up her nose, like she smelled something fool as her fingers traced the golden rim of the china she replaced to the glass shelving.

Maybe she should pick that particular pattern even if it was hideous just to piss the old hag off. After all, this was Judith's idea.

Haley begun by clearing her throat, more like stifled a giggle before she responded. "I actually like the one that's right in front of you, Judith." She was pleased with how nonchalant she sounded as she smothered a grin that threatened to split her face in half. That disgusted look on Judith's stunned face more than made up for the ugly pattern. A coy smile curved Judith's mouth as she slowly backed away from the china, holding her hands up in surrender. "It's your wedding, but please dear, call me mom."

Fat chance of that happening. Haley idly thought as she pushed back the sleeve of her green sage sweater to look at her watch. If she left now, she could get back to her house before Megan got home from school, get a shower and make it to work on time.

"Are you ready, Judi—I mean—" Swallowing hard, she met Judith's fond, sickening gaze, and pasted on a fake smile.

Why did she agree to marry Adam? Oh that's right. If she wanted to keep her daughter, she had no choice. "Mom." She said on a rushed breath, trying to filter the bitterness away. Judith clasped her hands together in glee.

"See? That wasn't that hard. Was it?" She cooed at Haley with a ridiculous grin on her face.

If she only knew, Haley dryly thought as she resisted the urge to roll her eyes. Apparently if you had mega-bucks like the old money bag strolling away from the exit insisted of towards it, you were expected to behave a certain way in the public eye. That meant no eye rolls, sticking your tongue out, or giving the finger. You know, all the fun stuff. She heard money made people do weird things, but this was just insane.

"What's the hurry, dear?" Judith nonchalantly asked as Haley trotted up next to her. From supposively being a bright lady back in her day, she was very dumb.

"I have to get ready for work." Haley stressed, politely of course. She didn't need to be scolded like a child again and be humiliated away from the public eye, like before.

"Oh that's nonsense." Judith started out as she waved away Haley's concern, like her job was beneath Judith, which it probably was. "Adam makes more than enough for you and my granddaughter." She continued with a careless shrug as she moved further into the wedding supply shop. This time she didn't resist the urge.

She earned a soft snicker from the shop attendant as she moved forward in hope she could get out of here on time. As it was, she wouldn't be able to get a shower and at this rate she wouldn't be able to give Megan a hug and kiss before the babysitter whisked her away. Mother-in-laws sucked. This one in particular.

"Hold the elevator, plea—" She called out as she sprinted towards the doors. "Ah shit!" She grumbled as she smacked her palms against the closed cool, stainless doors. Now she was going to have to take the stairs. "Thanks a lot, Judith." She crankily grumbled under her breath as she violently shoved the tan door open to the stairwell and begun to climb the steps to the fifth floor. Her pounding footsteps echoed off the walls of the quiet stairwell.

She was never doing this shit again no matter how much Judith complained or Adam bitched. *He* wasn't the one that had to deal with her whining all day long, now was he.

Second floor. Haley read the large plastic square and grumbled a little more. She began to reflect on Judith's bitter words from earlier in the day about her working. It was the same conversation she'd had with her son a few weeks ago. One that didn't go well. One that made her ignore him for a couple of days.

Adam of all people shouldn't be able to dictate what she did with her life. Maybe he could tell his goons that supported his Champaign trail what to do, but he couldn't tell her what to do and expect her to roll over and be his door mat. Don't think so Mr. Running-for-Governor, she thought smugly as she rounded the stairs to the third floor.

She didn't put herself through nursing school and raise Megan on her own for the first four years by working two dead-end job for nothing. While he traveled the globe, finding himself.

Puh-lease! There was nothing to be found. But, if he thought she was going to give that up, than he didn't know jack shit.

She couldn't believe she crazy enough to actually go along with this asinine plan of his. But she loved her daughter more than anything. That saying about parents walking through hell for their children. Yup. But instead of walking, it was more like she was being shoved.

The day she said "I do" to Adam Lucas, is the day she'd signed her soul over to the devil. Their marriage was not going to be based on love. More like it was going to be based on the other L word.

LIES. Adam had a 'situation' as he referred to it on more than one occasion, that he had to rectify.

Adam abandoned her when she got pregnant when she was just sixteen years old, saying it wasn't his child and that all she did was whore around. Four years and a paternity test, later he decides that he wants to run for Governor and suddenly he's by her side being the loving, dotting father.

How noble of him.

Too bad he couldn't have been that honorable when Megan was born and man up and help her out instead of letting her fall flat on her face.

At first Haley thought Adam had a change of heart, but the likihood of him having a kind heart would've been the same as her winning the lottery.

Not that great. But she gave him the benefit of the doubt and listened to why he was suddenly in her life, following her around like a shadow.

You know, that darken sensation that overcomes you sometimes, that gives you a gloomy feeling in the pit of your stomach, almost like a warning that something just isn't right. That was the feeling she had every time she was near Adam. She thought maybe she was just imagining things, being since he'd deceived her in the past. Her suspicions were confirmed when she discovered Adam's true intentions.

Sure, he wanted to be in his daughter's life. Which Haley had no problems with him being there for her. So what, if Adam and her had their differences and couldn't make it as a couple. That was no reason for Megan to be left growing up without a father. She knew what it was like to grow up without a father. Didn't parents want better for their children? Any loving parent would whole-hearty agree with that, expect when she found out why Adam took a sudden interest in Megan. For his own personal gain. He needed his *family* to support his run for Governor and proposed marriage, just for the sake of him being the good guy in the eye of the public. Noting more, nothing less.

A week after Megan was discharged from the hospital, Adam arrived at her house, unannounced of course and demanded she marry him. When she turned him down yet again, that's when Adam Lucas's true colors shone. He gave her an ultimatum, she'd either marry him, or risk losing her daughter for being a supposively unfit mother. He threatened the incident involving Megan being burned, he'd have the police records falsified, making it look like she intentionally hurt her if she didn't agree. He made it perfectly clear, child welfare would be involved within twenty-fours if she didn't agree, and he promised she'd never see Megan again.

Say what? He was blackmailing her? What other choice did she have?

Finally, the fifth floor. Haley let out a content sigh. She was never so glad to see something so good. She slowly swung the door open and headed towards the employee locker room to get ready for her shift.

"You look like you just ran a marathon." Tanya teased as Haley entered the locker room. She glared narrowly in Tanya's direction, but didn't say anything as she quickly moved over to the full length mirror in the corner past the wall of lockers and gasped. That old hag! Because of her diddling along in the shop she hadn't been able to get a shower, nor kiss her daughter. Now she looked like hell, her sweating hair clung to her face and—

She lifted her right arm and tucked her head down and took a few stiffs. And smelled like a gym sock. Paybacks sucked, Haley idly thought as she smeared on an extra layer of deodorant. As soon as her and Adam were married, she'd personally see to it that Judith was locked away to an old-farts home.

Not that she had anything against older people. Not all of them. Just one in particular. If she had to be prisoner to wedded abyss, then it should only be fair that Judith endure a generous helping of pureed prunes with every meal. She knew how much Judith despised them. All's fair in lies and war. Right?

"So what did Cruella complain about this time?" Tanya asked in a bored tone as she pulled out her chart and started her notes for the evening. That was the nickname given to her future monster-in-law not just because of the strong resemblance to the notorious villain, but also the way she laughed. More over Glenn Close, here comes Judith Lucas.

"Same ole', same ole'," Haley informed her in a equally bored tone as she too wrote in her charts. After a few moments of silence, except for the faint scrapping noises of the pen touching paper and the buzz of distant monitors bleeping, Tanya responded. "She's still on her high horse about you working."

"Yup." The P made a popping sound as Haley closed the chart and walked past the desk, over to the dry erase board and transferred patient's progress.

"Room 15 still didn't have her baby?" Haley asked incredulously as she looked up at Tanya with wide eyes. Tanya closed her eyes and gently nodded her head as she folded her arms across her pale yellow scrub shirt while she leaned her hip against the nurse's desk. "She's been in labor for thirty-six hours now." The melancholy was evident in Haley's voice as she turned back to her work in hand after mentally calculating Sarah's admission. Poor girl. Haley knew not only what it felt like to be in labor for a very long time, but also what it felt like to go through it alone. It was scary. She felt bad for the young girl but also felt a mild contentment that she hadn't giving birth yet.

# Chapter 3

"Wakey, wakey, sleepy head." Sounded a soft annoying voice. Maybe if he buried his head further under the pillow it would go away. Maybe it was just a bad dream? No such luck. He felt the mattress shift against him as he lay on his stomach.

Maybe it was Bruits, his brother's full grown German Sheppard, that he was forced into dog sitting. But dogs didn't talk. Did they? So it had to be—? He suddenly felt a warm hand glide across his bare back. Ah hell! Who in the hell did he bring home this time? The mystery woman's hand slipped under the covers that covered his naked ass and squeezed. Was it Janet? No, she's on vacation. Amber? No. She ended things with him two months ago. Julie? Oh holy shit! He needed to remember who in the hell was in bed with him and why. He never asked a woman to spend the night. Because that only lead to her getting crazy ideas in her head about wanting something more.

The only thing she'd get more of out of Brad Tyson was a good time.

He had to remember because for some reason if he called a woman by the wrong name he was the bad guy. Seriously? Women.

He slowly peeked one eye open and looked around. He wasn't being cautious because he still couldn't remember—? What in the hell was her name?

No, he kept his eyes open to a minimum because the sunlight pouring into his bedroom didn't exactly help a hang-over. His head pounded as he rolled to his back with his eyes pressed closed. Maybe if she spoke again, he'd know without having to open his eyes or pissing whoever it was off by guessing her name.

When the silence enveloped the room expect for their breathing, he was at a loss. He was just getting ready to open his mouth and say something to get her to talk but quickly shut it when the mysterious woman wrapped her hand around his shaft and begun to slowly stroke him.

Hmm? What is Heather? Felt like Heather's hands. Or maybe it could be Denise? Oh fuck he didn't know and right now he didn't give a shit. He let out a deep groan that rose from his throat. "You like that?" The mysterious woman purred with a smile on her face. He didn't have to open his eyes to know she was smiling, and who wouldn't be smiling with their hands wrapped around his thick, overly-abused member. He didn't recognize her voice though.

He mentally went through the woman he'd been with and checked all of them off his list. God! That list was longer than Santa's. He felt the bed shift again and a few seconds later he felt hair tickling his bare thigh followed by her warm breath feathering against his erection.

Maybe he should reconsider letting his one-night stands staying over? This could be beneficial to him. It had been a long time his he had morning sex. He almost forgot how much he liked it.

Nah! That would just compli—That was his last coherent thought as she wrapped her mouth around his aching erection and begun to suck. Now he knew who she was. Karen.

Well, this was awkward. Brad idly thought as he slouched on the wooden chair, bracing his elbow on the kitchen table, his chin balanced on his closed fist as he looked anywhere around the room expect into the eyes of the pissed of woman that frantically gathered her belongings. Turns out he'd been wrong when he thought he knew for sure who was giving him a blowjob. When the name "Karen" whispered past his lips through a moan, he knew the instant she pulled her warm, wet mouth away from him he was wrong. He tried to persuade her to finish what she started. That didn't go well either, as he rattled out the list of woman he'd slept with, in alphabetic order, hoping to say her name out loud. No such luck, and now he sat on his wooden chair with the worst case of blue balls known to mankind. This sucked.

"I can't believe after last night, you *still* don't know my name." Shouted Diane, making him wince as she snatched her panty hose from the back on the chair opposite him and shoved them in her purse. She finally had to tell him her name. When he practically begged, "Diane please don't leave he hanging." He casually pointed down with his pointer finger to the hard-on standing at attention. "You're an asshole," She screamed as she stormed out of his room, but not before throwing the closest thing she could find towards his head.

He ducked just in time to avoid being hurdle in the head with a thick, wooden picture frame of his favorite classic car. A 1969 fully-restored Chevy Camaro. He could've went into the bathroom and avoided her all together and took himself into his hand to relief the tension building, but he decided against that. He wanted to be near her. Not that he was feeling anything towards her. Good grief, no. He didn't want any more of his belonging to suffer at the hands of the revengeful woman from his stupidity.

When he heard the front door to his house slam shut, followed by the screeching of tires against the pavement, he scrubbed his hands against his face before dropping his hands to the table and letting out a frustrated sigh. He needed to stop his shit. Stop bringing random woman home with him.

He no longer took woman back to their homes ever since he had some woman's husband, that she inadvertently forgot to mention, threatening to kill him when he burst through their bedroom door. Brad quickly tossed the woman that was riding him like a cowboy off and scrambled to his feet and bolted out the door, naked with his clothes tucked in his arms. That was the day he was cited for 'indecent exposure'.

How was he suppose to know that a police officer lived next door to—? He couldn't even remember her name anymore. He really needed to stop this shit, before someone got hurt. Namely him.

# Chapter 4

"Thank-you so much for bringing her here." Haley's grateful tone had Pam, Megan's babysitter smiling sheepishly over her shoulder as she begun folding the pink Barbie fleece blanket she covered up with moments ago, when Haley entered her home after working over her scheduled shift.

She didn't like putting Pam on the spot by asking if she could bring Megan home so that way she could sleep in her own bed without her sleep being disturbed.

When Pam had asked if everything was okay, Haley was touched by the concern in her voice. Pam was like the mother Haley didn't and wouldn't have. Her own mother abandoned her when she found out she was pregnant with Megan. To be left alone at the age of sixteen to care for herself and an unborn child was the most scariest time of her life. That's why it was so important for her to be with Sarah tonight. As soon as Haley told Pam what was going on, Pam reassured her to stay as long as she needed. Pam was one of the few people that Haley trusted to look after Megan. She reassured Haley that she'd never find a trace of alcohol in her system, because she was allergic to the stuff. She also knew about being abandoned when she was younger by her mother and Adam and also knew why she was marrying Adam. Pam wasn't one to pass judgment, but she would voice her opinion. She told Haley she feared she was making the best mistake of her life and that marriage was a serious commitment. The only other person that knew was her best friend, Tanya. And she threatened to have her head examined. Haley knew she was making a huge mistake, but she couldn't risk losing the one thing that meant the most to her. Megan. Not again.

"How are they doing?" Pam asked as she busied herself filling the tea kettle with water and walking the pot over to the stove for it to warm. "Mason's doing very well. He's such a cutie." Haley gushed. "Sarah's doing well too, although a little sore."

"Oh?" Pam asked in concern as she pulled a chair out and sat at the oval dining room table across from Haley. Her thin white eyebrow drew together, gesturing her confusion. "She had to have a c-section." Haley solemnly replied. She'd never forget the look of fear that washed over Sarah's face when Dr. Carson announced the new birth plan. Haley grabbed her shaky hand and squeezed. Sarah looked up at Haley, tears begun to pool in her big, terrified brown eyes. "I'm so scared. Is the baby going to be okay?" Her voice trembling as she spoke. Haley sat on the chair next to her bed and looked at her straight in the eye and reassured her in her motherly tone. "Everything's going to be just fine." She whispered as she brushed the brown dampened curls that clung to Sarah's forehead away. Twenty minutes after being transported to the O.R. Sarah welcomed a happy, healthy, little boy into the world.

"That was so nice you could be there for her tonight." Haley looked over at Pam and brushed away a tear that she didn't realize had fallen. "I'm so proud of you." Pam boosted a few moments later as she slide her hands across the table giving Haley a fond smile as she squeezed her hand, enforcing her endearment. Haley smiled through the tears that wouldn't let up.

After Pam left for the night Haley rinsed out the cups they used for tea and loaded them into the dishwasher and set out to check on Megan before grabbing a shower and heading to bed. She'd check on Sarah and Mason in the morning, even though she didn't work tomorrow.

Haley had just adjusted the pink bedspread across her sleeping daughter's chest when the phone rang. Being careful to tip-toe out of the bedroom, she hurriedly darted to her room to silence the ringing.

"Hello?"

"It's about time you get your ass home and be a fucking mother to my daughter." Growled the person on the other end of the phone. He was drunk. No big surprise there. She really starting to wonder if he was born with a bottle of whiskey in his hands.

She let out a frustrated sigh as she closed her eyes and pinched the bridge of her nose. "If this is all your doing to do, I'm hanging up the phone. I've had a long day and I'm not in the mood for—" Haley sternly informed Adam as she gathered her yellow two-piece pajama set to dress in after her shower.

"Yes!" Adam interrupted as hissed into her ear. "I heard about you playing up the part of Florence Nightingale to some little whore that couldn't keep her legs closed." Haley could feel her temper starting to flare. She licked her lower lip, trying to quell her anger as she splayed her fingers against her hip with one hand, while her fingers of her other hand curled tightly around the phone.

"You don't know shit!" She retorted icily. How did he know about Sarah anyways?

His sharp intake of breath and the nasty chuckle that resonated through the phone had rage rippling along her spine. "I know a whore when I see one." His caustic words made her flush in shame.

"I'm sure you do." She was almost certain he'd heard the bridled anger in her voice. She wasn't directing her angry retort towards herself, but the other woman Adam had been sleeping with since they engaged.

Terrible regrets began to assail her when she thought back to the night she'd told him she was pregnant with Megan. He didn't say another word as he disconnected the call, leaving her to hear a dial tone. She pressed the end button, tossed the phone on the bed, making it bounce a few times before grabbing her clothing and storming off to the shower.

At first he was thrilled at the prospect of being a father and he couldn't wait to share a life with Haley and their unborn child. She was so relieved that he took the news well, being since he was leaving for college in the fall to study law. He reassured her everything was going to be alright. Haley reflected the sweet memories as the warm water cascaded a long her tired and tensed body.

She breathed a sigh of relieve before she went and told her mother the news. She knew she wasn't going to get the same reaction out of her as she did Adam, but she could hope.

Her mother's venomous words still pierced her heart after all these years. "You got pregnant on purpose just to trap the rich bastard. Didn't you?! You little tramp!" Her mother sneered as she busied herself in the kitchen, doing something. It happened so long along Haley had forgotten the things happening in the background of the small trailer they lived in. As Haley fought back the tears that threatened to spill down her flamed cheeks she hung her head solemnly as she strolled to her bedroom. "You can't stay here." She bit out harshly as she blocked Haley from entering her room.

"Why?" Haley asked, her voice trembling. That was the first and the last time her mother ever raised a hand to her. Haley ran out of the trailer with only the clothes of her back, crying hysterically as she clutched her red, swollen cheek. She never saw her mother again. As long as she had Adam to lean on, she could get through anything.

Haley scrubbed her body with such vigor, that her pink skin stung under the spray of water. As she realized what she had been doing to herself, the loofa slipped from her trembling hands as she raised her them to her face to silence her sobs and pressed her back against the cool, damp wall. She pulled her knees up to her chest when she felt the cool ceramic against her butt, as deep sobs racked her insides. She stayed like that until the spray of water trickling down to her toes turned cool.

"Mommy, can I have the marshmallow cereal with chocolate milk?" Megan asked excitedly as she bounced in her chair, waiting for Haley's response. Haley grabbed the red cardboard box from the pantry and pushed the door shut with her foot before opening the cupboard door above the sink and reached inside for two cereal bowl.

"How about white milk?" Haley suggested as pale cream pieces of cereal began clanging into the bowl as she poured it out. "No! Chocolate milk." Megan protested as she still bounced in her seat. "I think you're hyper enough this morning. What do you think?" She asked her daughter with her back towards her as she opened the refrigerator door and wrapped her hand around the handle of the gallon jug of white milk.

"Mommy? What does hyper mean?" Haley stopped her movements as she looked over to her daughter. Her messy chestnut shaded hair lay over her tiny shoulders. Her green eyes searched Haley's face for an answer as her left eyebrow drew up, waiting for a response. That was the one and only thing she'd gotten from Adam, everything thing else was just like her. Thank God!

"It means having way too much energy first thing in the morning." Haley playfully explained as her fingertips poked Megan's belly, tickling her. Haley was relieved that Megan no longer winced from the discomfort of her burns. She let out the most adorable giggle that could melt the coldest of hearts. Judith being the exception to that rule of course.

"Go get dressed." Haley said to Megan as she helped her from the table after they finished their breakfast together and playfully swatted her butt as she ran back to her bedroom shrieking with glee. Haley watched as Megan disappeared into her room and shook her head in amusement and smiled a fond, motherly smile as the image of Megan's long hair flowed carelessly around her as she ran. As crazy as it sounded, she knew she was doing the right thing by marrying Adam. Wasn't she? The ringing of the phone pulled her attention from her forlorn thoughts, over to the opposite doorway. A twist of agony knotted in her stomach as she neared it. This time she was checking the caller ID before she did anything.

The hospital?

"Hello?" She hoped they weren't calling her in. She had a day of fun activities planned out for Megan and herself.

"Hey! I just got off the phone with my cousin." Tanya started out in a chipper tone.

"Okay?"

"You know, the one that lives in Tennessee." Tanya clarified.

"Oh yeah. What's her name?" Haley screwed her eyes shut as she pressed the palm of her hand against her forehead, trying to remember the girls name.

"Heidi." Tanya drew the name out, followed by a soft chuckle a few moments later.

Haley's eyes sprung open as soon as she heard the name. "Heidi! That's right."

"Okay, well she's getting married and I've been invited to her wedding." Tanya informed her. The eagerness in her voice had Haley baffled. Yeah so? People got married all the time. What was so great about Tennessee?

"She's not getting married in her home state, though." Tanya said as if on cue, answering Haley's unspoken question. It was odd that Tanya had the ability to do that. It wasn't the first time and certainly wouldn't be the last either.

"Okay? So where's this blissful event taking place then?" She asked in mock enthusiasm.

"Are you ready for this?" Tanya was never one to just get to the point. No. She liked to drag things out as long as possible or until Haley playfully threatened to hang up on her. Whichever one came first.

"Vegas!"

"Vegas?"

"Vegas! And since I've been invited, I'm aloud to take a guest with me. So, how soon can you pack?"

# Chapter 5

"Hey, Brad?" Brad shifted his weight and leaned to the side as he rested his elbows on the frame of the car he was currently working on and peeked around the side of the raised hood in the direction of his boss's voice, and jutted his chin. Jerry, the owner of the garage stood in the doorframe and gestured for Brad to come in. Brad stood up and rolled his neck a couple of times, trying to loosen the strain on his aching muscles as he grabbed the tarnished rag that was spotted like a Dalmatian, and started to wipe his hands clean as he strolled towards the office.

He hesitated in the doorway when he'd noticed Jerry was seated behind his desk and on the phone. He motioned for Brad to take a seat as he continued to his conservation.

Brad nodded his head and sat in the only chair in the office, expect for the one Jerry was currently occupying, and looked around the office. Not trying to eavesdrop, but it was hard not to. Brad could only guess the one sided conservation had to deal with ordering car parts.

So he decided to distract himself by looking around the cluttered room. Various framed pictures lined the pale white walls of the small office. There were different pictures of Jerry shaking hands with Nascar legend, Richard Petty at various race tracks. Other pictures lined the walls of Jerry's—family?

Wait a minute. Was that Amy? Oh God! He hoped that she wasn't Jerry's daughter or for that matter, not somehow related to him. Is this why he was being called into the office? Oh shit. He didn't need to get his ass fired. He slouched in his chair as his eyes darted nervously from the picture to Jerry and then vice versa. She did kind of resemble him.

Fuck! So much for the distraction.

Wait. He never told Amy what he did for a living. He was safe. He could feel his shoulder start to sag with relief as he pushed upright in his chair, feeling more confident. That was until Jerry placed the cordless phone back on the cradle and caught his eyes flicking back and forth.

Oh fuck. Here it comes. He took a deep breath as Jerry clasped his hands together on the pile of paper resting in front of him, inclining his head and peering up at the picture of the young red headed girl, fondly. He was so busted. He swallowed hard as Jerry turned his attention to him, and smiled. *He'd play it cool.* He smiled back.

"That there is my little girl." Jerry announced proudly as he smiled at the picture like she was smiling back at him, which she sort of was.

Brad turned his head and looked at the picture like he'd never seen the woman before.

"Do you have kids, Tyson?" Jerry asked without looking up at him as he sorted through a stack of papers on his desk.

Him? Kids? No freaking way. "No, sir." He answered honestly. Where was he going with this? Jerry laughed without humor as he continued to sort through his stack. "Consider yourself lucky then."

Lucky? What in the hell was that suppose to mean?

"Here it is." Jerry announced as he restacked the massive pile of papers. As he read over the paper he spoke to Brad, candidly. "When a fine looking fella like yourself settles down and starts a family, pray you have all boys."

Okay. He called him into the office to talk about something that was never going to happen? He wished Jerry would just cut the bullshit and get right to it.

"Why's that, sir?" He curiously asked as he shifted around in the chair, suddenly he was feeling very uncomfortable.

"Well, ya see son." He started out as he adjusted his posture in the chair. "When you have boys you only have to worry about one dick. But when you have girls . . ." he paused and ran his fingers through his thinning grayish-brown hair and let out a troubled sigh. "You have to worry about every dick." He tossed the paper he was just holding and sat back in his chair nodding his head as he studied Brad's reaction to what he just said.

What could he say? *Sorry, sir. I didn't know she was your daughter.* Yeah. That would go over like a lead balloon. So he decided to nod along like he understood.

As the awkward silence seemed to stretch for hours Brad finally opened his mouth. "Is there a reason why you called me in here, sir?" Brad managed to keep his voice casual.

It was like Jerry was in some kind of trance or something that altered his thinking. "Huh?" He cocked his head to the side as his eyebrows drew together and stared at

Brad. Then the light bulb went on. "Oh yeah! Here." Jerry's puzzled expression relaxed as he leaned over the desk and handed Brad a paper before settling back into his chair. After a few moments of reading the paper, Brad lowered the sheet to his lap. "When do I leave?"

Jerry drew in a deep breath through his nose as he swiveled his chair and flipped the page to the calendar. "Next weekend sound good to you?" He asked as he turned back to face Brad.

"Yeah, that sounds good." He said trying to calm the eagerness in his voice. Anything sounded good right now, as long as he wasn't being shit canned.

"I'll have Amy make the arrangements." He informed Brad with a smile. Brad felt his stomach drop. It was the same woman he had a one night stand with. Shit. Suddenly he needed to know something. "Will you and your family becoming to the conference?"

He scoffed as a remorseful smile tipped his mouth. "Afraid not. Amy will be helping out here next weekend though. You know filing and that sort of thing." He said gesturing to the mound of papers covering his desk.

He smiled to his relief. Thank god he'd be in Vegas next weekend.

"Enjoy your stay, sir." The blond haired receptionist informed him sweetly as she licked her bottom lip seductively while her eyes freely roamed his body.

"Thanks." His tone was friendly, but not too friendly to encourage her as he grabbed his key card from the marbled counter and then slung his black luggage strap over his shoulder and headed towards the bank of elevators. He was turning over a new leaf, so to speak. He realized the day that—? What the hell was her name?

Hell. He couldn't remember and that's why he needed to change his womanizing days. It's something that his mother would love to hear, but she wouldn't hear it from him. No way.

"Meeooww! You can tell someone's in heat." Teased Evan, his best friend and co-worker from the garage as he clamped his hand down on Brad's shoulder. "Shut up!" Brad drew out in a playfully grumble as he elbowed Evan in the ribs.

"I'd do her." Keith bluntly announced as he pressed the white glowing button, summoning the elevator with a knowing smirk curving his mouth. Evan rolled his eye unconcerned. "Of course you'd do her. She has a heartbeat. Doesn't she?"

"Hey? What's that suppose to mean?" Keith's cranky snap earned howls of laughter from both Brad and Evan as the three entered the elevator.

"Dude," Evan started out as he wiped tears from his eyes with the pads of his fingers before clamping his hand down on Keith's shoulder. "It just means you're not picky. Now take our boy Brad here." Evan motioned his hand towards Brad and watched as Keith looked Brad's way. "He's picky. You know as well as I do if he wanted in the receptionist's panties, he'd be in them. You know what I mean?" As Evan finished his lecture he folded his arms across his chest and glared at Keith, almost like he was challenging him to say something to dispute his theory.

The rest of the ride to the sixth floor was in silence. Thank god. Brad didn't think he could handle anymore bullshit coming from Keith's mouth without putting his fist into it. He was so full of shit half the time when he talked about different woman he bedded. Evan knew it too, but decided not to say anything different to Keith. Some men just needed the ego boost he supposed.

# Chapter 6

"Ah! This is just what I needed." Brad informed his friend's as he flopped down on the couch in the hotel room twisting the cap from his bottle of MGD and lifting it to his lips, as a content smile curved his mouth. He needed to clear his mind of woman and concentrate on what was important.

This seminar. The garage he worked for was having some kind of seminar on the latest advances of foreign car parts. The seminar was suppose to prove that imports are better than American made.

Puh-lease.

There was no way imports were better than then American. On the contrary, statistics have shown that while American made is more expensive then foreign, over time American made is more durable and longer lasting than imported and the products overall safety in greater than domestic parts. That is what this meeting was all about . . . tomorrow.

Right now, him and his friend's had the rest of the evening to do as they pleased.

"Come on man," Keith complained for the third time since they all entered the room. "Where in Vegas for Christ sake. Do you know how many woman are just waiting to get a piece of this." Keith illustrated his point by pointing to his crotch.

"Yeah, maybe if she carries around tweezers with her, needle dick." Evan slapped his hand down on his leg and burst out laughing as Keith narrowed his murderous glare at Brad. "That bitch didn't know what she was talking about." Keith countered a few moments later as he puffed out his chest. "Besides, we were in the back seat of her car in the dark. She only seen the shadow of it before she opened the door and left." He continued as he lifted his brown bottle to his lips and took a long pull.

Keith was one of the other mechanics at the garage. He was really a hard worker and knew a shitload about car repairs. But the passion he had towards cars lacked when it came to woman.

Yeah, he was no better when it came to woman, but he was changing that and knew better than to outright say to a woman "that dress looks nice, but it would look better laying on my floor." There was just some things you never say to a woman and that's one of them. Keith found out more than once, when different woman smacked him across the face, poured beer over him, or he'd been chased out of a bar by some woman's very pissed off boyfriend.

Brad took another sip of his beer before resting his head against the back of the overstuffed couch and closed his eyes. He didn't come to Vegas to look for a woman, but if he happened to come across one maybe he'd really apply himself this time and try to make things work. He could see himself married, not in the near future or anything like that, but it could happen. He wasn't getting any younger. Then there'd be . . . kids? His eyes few open as and he began to shift around on the couch suddenly uncomfortable of where his thoughts were leading him.

Sure, he loved kids. He spoiled all five of his nephews like crazy. But he could do that. He was the Uncle. But to have kids of his own that would mean . . . ? That would mean that he'd have to think about someone else's well being, besides his own.

And what if he had a daughter? He'd have to keep guys away from his little girl. Guys like himself. Jerry's words picked that moment to filter through his mind. Great! Just, fucking great! He glumly thought as he raised his bottle to his lips and drained it.

"If you guys want to stay here and continued the slumber party, fine." Keith bit out as he rose from his chair. "But I'm going out and showing these Vegas girls what they've been missing." He informed his friends as his hand reached for the door knob.

"Don't forget the tweezers." Brad teased in a sing song voice. Keith halted his steps inside the open door, leading into the hallway, with his back towards Brad, and Evan. His body visible tensing as his hand tightened on the door knob before he stepped outside of the room. Brad and Evan burst out laughing as Keith grumbled something under his breath before slamming the door shut behind him.

Haley suddenly awoke to what sounded like someone heavily pounding on the hotel room door. She quickly sat up in bed and looked around the semi-dark room. Was she dreaming? She sleepily thought as she tried to focus her hazy vision towards the noise.

"Is someone at the door?", Tanya whispered from the loft above as she rubbed the corners of her eyes. Haley looked up at her friend and shrugged her shoulders dubiously. Tanya's long blond hair hung over her shoulders as she leaned her hands on the confines that enclosed the open loft as she silently yawned. After a few moments of silence, Haley looked back up towards Tanya as they both shrugged their shoulder. Tanya moved away from the wall as Haley repositioned her pillow getting ready to lay back down, when the pounded sounded again followed by incoherent mumbling.

"That's it!" Tanya snapped as she flipped the light switch before stomping down the steps towards the door. Haley blinked a few times as her eyes adjusted to the light before she made her way over to the door. Without even looking through the peephole, Tanya's fingers made quick work of unlocking the door as she yanked it open. "Tanya!" Haley scolded in a hushed tone as she shook her head in disbelief. Tanya glared at her as she yanked the door back. Tanya was not a person to reckon with before she either had her coffee or if she was woken before she was ready to be awake.

"What!" Tanya yelled as she flung the door open and came upon a blond haired man standing at the door with both of his thick forearms resting on the doorframe, trying to hold him up. He was obviously drunk and lost. Haley all most felt sorry for him. Almost.

"I forgot my ke—" The drunk guy started out as he swayed back and forth. "Well, hello gorgeous," he slurred as lips twitched and his brown eyes widen, devouring Tanya's chest. Tanya was dressed in a pale blue camisole top and matching boy shorts when she flung the door open. The drunk guys eyes raked over Tanya's body from head to toe as a wicked unnerving grin crept up his stubble coated face. "Are you happy to see me?" He continued to slur as he reached out his hand and pointed to Tanya's chest. Haley knew without a doubt what the sicko was referring to. Tanya's hand shot out and smacked the drunk guys hand away. "Hey, that wasn't nice." He sweetly scolded Tanya as he grabbed a hold of the doorframe to steady his large frame and took an unbalanced step towards her. Haley felt her heart rate pick up the pace. This guy could very easily manhandle Tanya. He partially towered over her.

"Oh Yeah!" Tanya irritability countered as her hands clenched into fist by her sides.

"Yeah," he slurred again as his brown eyes continued to search every curve of her body. A creepy grin tipping his mouth. Haley's movement caused him to look over Tanya's shoulder towards Haley as he licked his lips as he took another uncalculated step, only to be stop as Tanya blocked his path.

"I'm not a nice person!" Tanya seethed between clenched teeth as she drew back her fist and punched the drunk guy in the face. Haley's hands shot up to her face as she gasped. He stumbled back a few steps as he leaned over and cupped his face before Tanya slammed the door with such a force. The pictures on the wall inside the living room rattled. A quick snap of her wrist and the door was locked again.

"You bitch," the drunk guy shouted from behind the closed door. "You broke my nose." He slurred while still outside of their room. "He's lucky that's the only thing I broke." Tanya grumbled a few moments later as she continued to calm herself down by taking long, deep breaths as she leaned her head against the back of the couch with her eyes closed.

Haley tiptoed over to the door and peeked out through the peephole when they didn't hear any more profanities from the drunk guy.

"He's gone." Haley whispered as she sat down next to her best friend and let out a deep sigh. Their silence quickly faded as the pounding on the door started again. Tanya's eyes snapped open, her eyes narrowing as she quickly got to her feet and stormed over to the door. Once again, she didn't even bother looking before she flung the door open. Haley was hot on her heels as their door swung open.

"What?!" Tanya demanded again.

Two guys gasped and took a cautious step back as both of their arms flew up in surrender. Blue, and brown eyes widen at Tanya's less than subtle greeting.

"Uh . . ." The first guy started out as he looked around nervously with his thick tanned arms still up. Haley noted some kind of tattoo was on the inside of his forearm. He lowered his arms slowly, which made it difficult for her to get a good like at it anymore, as he cleared his throat. "I'm sorry about my friend." He started, his pleading blue eyes bored into Tanya, seeking empathy while gesturing down the hall with his thumb and swallowed loudly. "He forgot his key and um . . ." His voice trailed off as he elbowed the other guy in the ribs that was trying to hold back a laugh. Haley eyes moved from the sandy blond headed guy to the other one as her breath caught in her chest. He was gorgeous.

Well they were both good looking. But the dark haired guy gorgeous. Not just model gorgeous, but bad boy gorgeous. He ran his hands through his dark, waving hair as he stared aimlessly to the ceiling. An irresistible dimple indented his cheek as he smiled at his friend's apologetic groveling. He finally looked away from the ceiling. Amusement danced in his deep, dark, mocha eyes. "What my friend here is trying to say." The bay boy hottie started out as he clamped a thick hand onto his friend's wide shoulder and smiled at Tanya.

His deep voice sounded thick with sleep. Maybe he too was woken up by his friend's overactive libido. It didn't matter though, just as long as he kept talking. The sound of his voice made something inside Haley catch fire. He continued to talk about his friend, but Haley quit paying attention to what he was saying as her eyes raked over the white wife beater that strained against the bumps and ridges of his burly chest and made his tanned completion glow, down to the worn, faded Levi's that clung to his bulky legs. A small split in the denim running parallel near his zipper suddenly had her fingers itching to poke around in that hole.

Deep, rich, laughter suddenly pulled her attention from the man she was visually propping. A strange, faint fervent looked flashed in his eyes as her gaze meet his. She felt an eager affection coming from him as he seductively looked her over. Her pulse leapt with excitement as he beamed with approval. For some reason she wanted him to find her desirable.

Without notice the, the enticing glint in his gaze was suddenly clouded over with dismay. She dropped her lashes quickly to hide the hurt, as she tried to ignore the mocking voice inside her head that wondered why.

Why he suddenly look at her repulsively?

"He's an asshole and I'm sorry that he disturbed you nice ladies. Have a good night." His tone was very clipped. He turned on his heels and walked away as fast as his long legs could take him without looking back. His mood switched from laid back to . . . ? She didn't know, but it felt odd. Very odd. The fire she felt just moments ago that was raging inside of her was quickly doused with rejection.

# Chapter 7

"Has anybody ever told you how annoying you are?" Keith grumbled sleepily into the pillow as he rolled over onto his side, away from Brad and burrowed further under the covers on the couch.

"Rise and shine sleeping beauty." Brad said with a grin as he ripped the covers off Keith in one fluid movement and laughed to himself when Keith grumbled more as he tried reaching his arm behind himself, blindly searching for the covers and fell on to the floor with a loud thud.

"You're a dick." Keith complained through frown as he scooted against the bottom of the couch and drew his legs up to rest his elbows on his knees as he ran his hands threw he tousled hair while squinted against the light.

"Takes one to know one." Brad countered gruffly as he moved towards the kitchenette and swiped his Styrofoam cup from the counter and swallowed down the last of his coffee in one gulp before tossing it into the trash can.

"What the hell's your problem?" Keith mumbled as he got to his feet and stumbled a couple of times to the counter. He rested his elbows on the marble as he continued to squint against the light shining into the room. Dark circles rested under his blood shot eyes. The circles had nothing to do with lack of sleep, and everything to do with being punched in the face. His nose was still swollen.

"You're my problem." Brad spat out. "We have a seminar in a couple of hours and your still fucking hung over." Brad said as he gestured wildly towards Keith slumped body partially laying on the counter.

"Stop yelling." Keith mumbled as he laid his head against the marble. Brad narrowed his glare and stared at his friend as his fist clenched open and shut by his sides. Just when Evan and himself put their necks and careers on the line for Keith; telling their boss that Keith is a 'good guy' and they'd make sure he stayed in line along with Keith's promise, this is the thanks they get out of it? What an idiot. Brad idly thought as he ran his hands through his hair in frustration.

"You know, you're lucky those girls didn't call the cops on you last night." Evan sternly informed Keith as he pointed an accusing finger at him, while strolling over to the coffee maker.

Keith slowly picked up his head and blinked his eyes a few times before pushing himself away from the counter and standing upright. Or as best as he could. "Those girls wanted me last night." He smugly mumbled as he blinked his eyes a few times while gently nodded his head as he absently stared over Brad's shoulder, like he was reminiscing a good memory or something.

How pathetic was that? Brad thought dryly.

"Yeah, I'm sure there was a lot the blond haired girl wanted to do to you." Evan said sarcastically as he tossed his cup into the trash and he chuckled.

"No. Not her." Keith grumbled as he waved Evan's response off. He still had the same smug look on his face as he continued to stare into outer space. "She's too feisty anyways. I'm talking about the brunette with the big nipples that poked out from her top, begging for my attention, until that blond bitch got in the way." Keith sneered at the bitter memory as an ugly twist of disgust consumed him.

Brad's hands clenched into fist by his sides as his nostrils flared with—Anger?

Why in the hell should it bother him listening to the ridiculous bullshit lies flying from his mouth? That's all it was, was lies. But for some reason it still pissed him off. He didn't want Keith talking about her, nor going anywhere near her.

He felt still body stiffen. Where the hell did that thought come from? What the hell was wrong with him?

"Dude?" Evan whispered to Brad as he leaned over to his ear.

"Hmm?" Brad responded as he looked over to Evan.

"What's up with you?" Evan questioned as he jutted his chin towards Brad's fist with a perplexed expression.

Yeah? Good question? Now if he could try to tell Evan something to pacify him, instead of the truth. He couldn't tell his best friend that he wanted to push her against the wall to run his tongue from her lips to her toes. He was suppose to be making a change for the better. Right? And if he did that, what would that make him look like?

A man. The part of his mind that didn't like logic interfering, implored. But the rational part of his mind wanted to stay clear of her. This was the new Brad. Not that he wasn't attracted to her, because he was. His raging hard-on almost made that evident last night when he adverted his eyes elsewhere and quickly high tailed it back to their room. He was always think with the head between his legs and look where that has gotten him so far. No, the new Brad that wasn't going to sleep with random woman anymore, as tempting as she was. He needed to stay away from her. But, he also didn't want Keith anywhere near her.

"I'm just tired of always having to cover Keith's ass." Brad gestured towards Keith's slumped body laying on the counter, with a puddle of drool forming on the marble. Evan slowly shook his head in disbelief "If you say so." He said sounded unconvinced.

Yeah. He did say so. Just as long as Keith left her alone and he didn't happen to run into her again. Then he wasn't so sure about his new found concepts.

# Chapter 8

Haley dressed in a spaghetti strap sundress with a combination of deep and soft shades of cream, set off the white hibiscus accented in blue, beautifully. She made her way over to the mirror and glanced at herself one more time, before deciding on the dress she had on for certain. A generous amount of cleavage peeked out from the top of her dress and along with the other five dresses she tried on.

What did she expect? It's the price you pay for having a child, she supposed as she gave a careless shrug before smoothing her hand down the front of her dress. Besides, this dress was the best option, it was hot outside after all. And it was only going to get hotter. It was March of crying out loud and they were in Vegas were the temperature was already flirting in the nineties at nine o'clock in the morning. The forecast predicted that by early afternoon, records could be broken from the unusually warm weather for this time of year.

"You look nice." Tanya's compliment should have put a smile on her face, but it didn't. She didn't feel nice. Haley looked over her shoulder towards her best friend and grumbled to herself. Tanya looked her flawless self in her tan sundress, matching Haley's, expect for the ample cleavage. They went shopping before the wedding was to take place and bought something nice to wear. Tanya demanded Haley buy the outfit she had on right now, claiming it showed off all of her curves, and it did, but she still felt invisible around Tanya sometimes. Like last night.

The most gorgeous man she'd ever lay eyes on wouldn't even look at her again. He focused his attention on Tanya. Just like all the other guys did whenever they went out somewhere together. She scoffed to herself. The only attention she could get was from Adam, when he was drunk and that really wasn't the kind of attention any woman wanted. She inwardly cringed. The only attention she could get was from her drunk fake fiancé.

Tanya gasped as her eyes widen. "What?" Haley asked as eyebrows drew together in confusion. "I'll be right back."

Tanya said brightly as she marched up the steps. A few moments later Tanya strolled down the steps and headed straight for Haley.

"What are you doing?" Haley asked, sounding unsure as Tanya stood behind her and pulled her chestnut shaded hair to the side as her arms rose over Haley's head. "You'll see." Tanya replied, sweetly.

"There." Tanya said as she gently pushed on Haley's shoulder, gesturing from her to turn and face her. "It matches your eyes." Tanya said fondly as a smile curved her mouth as she brushed the hair from Haley's shoulder. Haley's hand shot up to her neck as her thumb and pointer finger rolled around the pendant.

"Go look at it." Tanya said eagerly as her hand gestured towards the bathroom. Haley flipped the switch and blinked a few times against the bright light as she moved closer to the large mirror. When her eyes focused she gasped and stormed out of the bathroom.

"I thought you were buying this for yourself?" She asked in a curious, stern tone.

"Would you have let me buy it for you?" Tanya's sculptured brow rose up her forehead as she looked at Haley, waiting for the challenge.

Haley didn't even hesitant. "No."

"I seen how much you liked it and your my best friend." Tanya said sweetly as she neared Haley and wrapped her arms around her as a twist of guilt swirled in her stomach. Now she felt even worse than she did before. Not only did Tanya radiate beauty on the outside, it also shone from within.

"Ready to get this over with?" Tanya asked a few moments later as she pulled away from Haley. "Yeah." Haley quickly said over her shoulder as she brushed away the tears that threatened to give her away.

"Are you crying?"

"Of course not." Haley said through a smile as she turned towards her friend. "What made you think that?"

"Oh. I don't know. Maybe the way your voice broke."

"It's silly." Haley said as she adverted her eyes to the floor and casually waved off Tanya's inquiry.

"Honey. You're not on the ugly duckling kick again are you?" There was sincere concern in Tanya's voice as she searched Haley's eyes for an answer when she looked into Tanya's dark brown eyes. Haley sheepishly nodded her head.

"What? What makes you say that?" Tanya politely demanded as they made their way to the couch. Haley plopped down first followed by Tanya as she waited for her response.

"When guys check you they smile in approval and practically follow you around like a love sick puppy. When they look my they frown, and run for the hills, like they can't get away from me fast enough." She shouldn't even be thinking about other man, since she was getting married. Ah Hell! How was she kidding? There was no way she was going to be doing anything intimate with Adam Lucas ever again.

"That's so not true."

"You don't have to lie to me to cheer me up."

"Haley Lynn Martinez! I can't believe you think that about yourself." Tanya shook her head in mock disbelief as her eyes implored her. "If you could only see what I see. You're a hottie and any guy would know that as soon as he looks at you."

Yeah sure. Haley thought dryly. Just like last night? She finally meet a man that made every part of her zing with desire just for him to look away from her like she grown a second head that threatened to bite him or something.

"Look at the guy from last night." Tanya started out as she shut the door behind them. "You mean the drunk guy?"

"No." She drew out the O. "That man should be the poster child for avoiding guys in bars, period. The other guy. The tall one." Haley thought about it for a few moments as she pushed the button for the elevator. "Which one? They were both tall."

Just then the bell lightly sounded as the elevator door slowly slide open. "That one." Tanya whispered

"Man, I'm starved." Complained Keith as he searched in the mini refrigerator tucked beneath the counter for the second time. "Maybe if your stupid ass wouldn't have gotten drunk last night you would've been able to attend the important seminar, that might I add provided lunch, you wouldn't be hungry. Would you?" Brad sternly implored as he aimlessly flipped through the channels.

"You're an asshole." Keith smugly grumbled as he walked past Brad and flopped down on the chair, next to the couch and grabbed his water bottle from the wooden end table and chugged it down.

Brad ignored Keith's words as he continued to search the channels. "Hey!" Evan complained around a mouthful of food. "I was watching that." He grumbled as he leaned towards Brad and ripped the remote from his hands and righted himself on the couch and flipped the channel back to the previous program.

"I told you. He's an asshole." Keith chimed in as he rested his head on the back on the chair with his eyes closed and his hands clasped against his chest. Brad continued to sit on the couch with his elbow resting on the arm and his chin balanced on his closed fist as he glared at Keith.

Because of that dumb ass, he had to lie through his teeth and let everyone at the meeting know that Keith wasn't feeling well and that's why he wasn't able to attend today's meeting. He was sick and tired of lying for him. But in the same sense he couldn't exactly tell his boss the truth because he promised Keith would behave. But that wasn't the only thing that pissed him off.

He saw her again. He didn't get much sleep the night before because every time he closed his eyes all he seen was her beautiful face. Those green eyes that looked like a tropical rainforest. When she looked up at him for the first time, it was like she was wasn't just seeing him. It was like she saw into his soul. Her hair looked like a long, shiny, chestnut waterfall, framing her soft, beautiful face. And her lips were full and appeared to be velvety soft. He idly wondered if her lips were as soft as they look. He was tempted to find out this morning when she entered the elevator. He had an instant hard-on when he seen her. It was the weirdest thing he ever experienced before. No woman ever turned him on that before with touching him. He wanted to peel that dress off of her and ran his tongue all over her body. And she smelled so damn good. Like some kind of berries. Just the thought her aroma had his cock twitching behind his zipper.

He let out a deep sigh as he stared up at the ceiling. He felt himself slipping back into his old habits. He needed to get laid. More importantly, he needed to find her. But he couldn't just go over and pound on her door and demand sex. Well, he could but he didn't want her to think he was desperate even though he was. Desperate for her. This was all Keith's fault, he inwardly grumbled to himself as he lifted his head and glared at the asshole again. If he wouldn't have went out and gotten himself drunk, he would've never known there was a cute little brunette next door.

"What the fuck was that for?" Keith sputtered out in a hoarse voice a few moments later as he coughed deeply and make choking sounds as he leaned over on the recliner chair with his head facing the floor.

"There! Now I'm an asshole!" Brad bit out gruffly as he walked towards the stairs. "You know . . ." Cough "I hate . . ." cough again "When you fli—" deep cough "Flick my throat." Gasp for air. "You ass—" really deep cough.

"Asshole." Keith called out. "I'll get you for that." His hoarse voice was making it difficult to yell at Brad.

"I'm sure you will." Brad whispered to himself as he climbed the steps to the loft and headed towards the bathroom with a satisfied smile on his face. He knew all too well what it felt like to be flicked in the Adam's apple. He did after all grew up with two brothers.

After his shower he was dressed in casual clothes and ready to get the hell out of this hotel room. Maybe he just needed to clear his head for awhile? Maybe he should find some random girl to fuck into oblivion, for old time's sakes until he forgot all about the brunette?

This was crazy, he idly thought as he stabbed the glowing button, summoning the elevator. He didn't even know her name. Was she married? Right now none that of mattered to him. It wasn't her name or marital status that he was concerned about right now. All he was concerned with was finding her and making sure she knew his name. That way she knew what name to scream as he drove her over the eroticized edge. Suddenly George Michael's lyrics thrummed in his mind as he entered the elevator about wanting sex.

# Chapter 9

When Evan and him first entered the bar they scanned the area, and seen the same random people they'd seen the night before when they had to pry Keith from the barstool. He was almost ready to turn around and walk out the door and head back to the room.

That was until he seen her sitting at the bar with her friend. Her shiny chestnut hair shimmered under the flashes of bright light. Her carefree smile lit up the dim room. He had to be near her. As he began to approach her, he watched Keith swoop in. Brad stood rooted to the floor, clenching his teeth, he was furious. A stab of jealously pierced his chest. He didn't know why, but it did. He knew he had no right to be jealous over a woman sitting next to man, unless that man just happened to be Keith.

He couldn't move over to the bar fast enough when he seen Keith's hand slithering up her bare thigh. Only he was allowed to touch her like that.

What the hell? He didn't know where that thought came from, but he'd deal with it later.

"I'm married!" Haley blurted out, out of frustration as she pushed the same creepy guy's, wondering hand away for the third time. Which it wasn't necessary a lie . . . He didn't need to know she wasn't married . . . . yet.

This was the same creepy guy that Tanya could've killed last night with her bare hands. Why couldn't she be in the same mood as yesterday?

God! The man couldn't take a hint when she already told him she wasn't interested in going back to his room with him. Tanya almost choked on her strawberry daiquiri when Haley announced her fake admission. Haley whipped her head in her friend's direction and seen the tears forming in her eyes as her shoulders trembled as she tried to hide her laughter.

"You okay?" Haley asked with mock concern as smile crept up her mouth from watching Tanya's reaction to her lie to the jerk that kept blowing in her ear.

Seriously? How was air being blown into one's ear suppose to be a turn-on?

"Hmm" Tanya hummed as tears trickled down her cheeks as she tried really hard to suppress her laughter as she vigorously nodded her head, gesturing she was fine. Haley slowly turned her attention back to the smug looking man. At least he finally removed his lips from her bare shoulder.

Swirls of red, blue, and yellow danced in his pale hazel eyes from the disco ball overhead. She didn't want to lie to the man, but he wasn't giving her any other choice.

When Tanya and her first entered the ultra trendy night club, named Sinners, she half expected to see cages with half clothed woman shaking their ass's or topless woman grinding provocatively against shiny poles. After all they were in Vegas. But to her surprise it was nothing what she'd expected. It was very descent. They scooped out the place before finally deciding to sit at the bar. Haley noticed the dance floor that reminded her of a giant chess board with glowing, flashing neon lights that alternated colors to the beat of the music.

A sofa rested against the side wall opposite the dance floor. The grayish-blue wall that was situated behind the sofa had swirls of bright colors that pulsed in time with the music. The images of twirling lights reminded her of a giant Spiro graph. The sofa and matching lounge chairs looked like they were inflatable and glowed like they were almost ultraviolet. They made their way over to the curved bar that also glowed like the rest of the furniture and plopped down on cushioned black stools. As they scanned their surroundings while waiting for their drinks, that's when creepy guy stood up from the glowing chair and waved his arm at Haley, trying to lure her over to him.

Yeah. Right. Like that was going to happen. She thought in disbelief as she slowly turned her attention back to the bar, pretending like she didn't see him. Which was kind of hard. If he would had glowing wands in his hands, like the ones they used on a runway, he could have easily maneuvered an airplane to land the way he was now franticly flailing his arms around.

"Don't look now." Warned Tanya in a hushed tone as she glared over Haley shoulder, in the direction of the creepy guy. "But here comes that creepy looking guy from last night." Great! Haley rolled her eyes and inwardly grumbled. He was the last person she wanted to see tonight.

Maybe if she just sat there and stared down at her drink, he'd walk on by.

Maybe he'd take her static posture as she wasn't interested in him. She could only hope. She'd cross her fingers and sent up a silent pray, urging him on to the next willing woman.

Apparently someone from above wasn't taking any request that day.

So an hour later, creepy guy still wasn't taking a hike after she already told him she was with some body.

"Hey! Stop it!" Haley demanded as she scooted closer to Tanya who was in deep conservation with some guy she meet when she went to the bathroom. She wished she would have meet someone, anyone. Just to get creepy guy to leave her alone. Haley bumped into Tanya's back as she pushed his hand away, again. Tanya was oblivious to Haley's movements.

Just great.

Haley was getting ready to open her mouth to Tanya to suggest going back to their room, when Tanya let out a giggle. Not just any giggle, but the kind of giggle that told Haley Tanya was into this guy and wasn't going to be leaving alone, or with her.

Super great!

"I told you I'm with someone!" She hissed as she pushed his hand away that was trying to climb under her dress.

"Oh yeah?" Mock enthusiasm filtered through his voice as he craned his neck to look around the dimly lit room. "I don't see anybody coming over to you, darling" He said without humor as a smile crept up his face revealing his bugs bunny teeth as he settled his arm around her shoulders and tried to grab a handful of her breast. She wiggled her herself to move his arm. "Enough!" She spat out as she started to stand up, only to quickly sat back down as the room begun to spin. She grabbed the edge of the bar and squeezed her eyes shut, willing the affects of too much alcohol to not take over. Not now. Not when this pervert had been groping her all night.

"She's with me." Rumbled a deep voice with an edge of intimidation. That's odd. The voice sounded a little familiar.

Haley whipped her alcohol soaked head in the direction of the deep, sexy voice and came eye level with a black t-shirt clinging to a rather large, tall, burly man, tucked inside another pair on faded Levi's. Stunned, she blinked a couple of times before slowly inclinging her head until she was looking into twinkling pools of simmering chocolate.

Her breath caught in her chest as she felt her heart starting to race as she bite the inside of her lip to fight back the moan of approval that threatened to escape.

He looked even better than he did this morning in his black business suit. And even then he looked pretty damn fine with a few buttons his white dress shirt open, exposing tanned, sculptured smoothness. Creepy guy scoffed as he moved closer to Haley, obvious threatened by her saviors appearance.

"Keith." The bad boy hottie warned the man named Keith with a glare of hostility. He slowly stood and puffed out his chest as he eyed the bad boy up, in a challenging way before he looked over his shoulder towards Haley. "I'll catch you later." He said as he winked.

Anger flared in his brown eyes. "No you won't." The bad boy warned, bridled anger in his voice, as he took Keith's vacant stool and wrapped his arm around Haley's waist and pulled her near. "She already has plans." He replied sharply. The warmth of his hand seeped through the thin material of her dress, creating a thrill of excitement to course through her along with the words he just spoke.

Keith's face paled with anger before he turned on his heel and stomped towards the exit. As Haley watched his retreating back as a pang misery crushed the feelings of elation from moments ago. Not that the he was leaving. She was glad to see him go, but that meant that her rescuer didn't need to stay by her side to keep him away.

He could go flirt with any woman he wanted to now. She should just go back to her room, alone before she got in over her head with the bad boy hottie.

"Thank-you." Haley mumbled as she grabbed her clutch purse from the bar and scooted towards the edge of her stool, in another attempt to leave.

"Your welcome?" He sounded unsure of himself as his eyebrows drew together in confusion as he searched her eyes for some kind of explanation as to why she was leaving.

Like she could tell him she found him drop dead gorgeous and wanted nothing more than to run her tongue all over him, but he was only here to send the creep away, so she decided against it. He only told Keith she was busy for the night to get him to leave. She might be a little drunk, but she wasn't stupid.

# Chapter 10

"Can I buy you a drink?" Brad asked out of sheer desperation. He pretty much knew the answer to that question, but he didn't want her to leave. He wanted to get to know her better. Really better.

He knew he'd probably regret his hormone-driven decision in the morning, but he'd deal with that then. She looked up at him and gave a sheepish smile before adverting her eyes down to her clenched hands. Was she nervous? Without a word, she nodded her head. Brad signaled for the bartender and ordered himself a MGD. "What are you having tonight?"

She looked up at him and brushed her hair behind her ear and licked her lips. His cock twitched at just the faint sight of her pink tongue poking out between her plump pink lips. There was a playful twinkle in her green eyes before she spoke. "You." Make that a full blown erection on her blunt admission. Maybe he wouldn't regret his choice come morning?

He leaned into closer to her and breathed in her scent. "Well then. I guess this is your lucky night." His voice was low and rumbled and it appeared a shudder of desire shot through her. He only hoped that's what it was. There was only one way to find out.

"Wanna get out of here?" He whispered as he raised his eyebrows suggestively and then jerked his heads towards the exit. She turned in her stool to face him as he did the same with her. He scooped her hands into his and slowly ran the pads of his thumbs across her knuckles. His body tingled from the light contact. The hitch in her breath told him everything he wanted to know before she slowly nodded her head. She too was feeling some kind of force from their brief contact.

She pulled away from him, just enough for her to lean back and whispered something in her friend's ear, making her friend's eyes dart across Haley's shoulder before her eyes widen as she stared at him.

Was she giving him the look of approval?

Before he could think too much about it, Haley turned back to him with a huge grin on her face. Her cheeks blazed a deep rose color. What exactly did she whisper to her friend that would make her blush? God! He couldn't wait to find out. She placed her clammy hand in his and once again he felt the same electric current he'd felt before when he touched her hand before.

He kept a hold of her hand as he wove them between the people that had begun to crowd the club. It looks like the woman that tried to seduce him earlier had finally meet someone else to tease. The woman had no shame obviously. Her hand was tucked inside Keith's pants and judging by the rapid movements around his crotch, he knew she was giving him a hand job out in the open.

What in the hell did she just say?

You?

That so not like her to say something as bold as that. It had to be the affects to too much alcohol. Yup. That's what it was. Liquid courage. That had to be it. Because she never talked to a man like that, especially on she just meet for the second time in less than twenty-four hours. What also didn't help the situation was the way his inviting brown eyes bored into her with silent expectation. Who was she to say no?

"I'm Brad, by the way." His voice rumbled as they neared the exit.

"Haley," she responded, hoping he heard her over the pulsing music. His hand was rough and calloused and sent a quiver of want deep inside her belly. Liquid heat begun to pool between her legs.

What the hell? It a small gesture. A casual greeting really. Besides, she'd touched numerous hands earlier in the day during Tanya's cousin's wedding and didn't feel anything remotely close to what she was feeling now. Which was a good thing.

She wouldn't want to make the prudish man from Tanya's family think she was into them and their snobbish ways. They greeted everyone at the wedding with admiration. That was until they seen Tanya and herself. Then they wrinkled their noses like they'd smelled something bad and frowned down at them in disgust.

If anyone should be feeling revolted, it should be her. First she had to deal with Adam's overbearing ways of why she was flying to Vegas. Like she needed his permission. Puh-lease!

She had to remind herself many times on the flight why marry Adam was a good thing. And then be forced to attend an outdoor wedding in the stifling heat was one thing. She got that. But for them to look down at her as if she was something they scrapped off the bottom of their hefty loafers? Seriously?

Her hand remained in his as the emerged from the club that had begun to become thick with heat. Not just heat from all the people that had gathered in there but heat from impending sex and sin. She wasn't naïve when it came to clubs like this. She knew what went on behind closed door even though it was not one of those clubs but still she wasn't dumb. The tall blond standing by the exit was proof of that. That's something she could never do. Make out with a guy in a public place.

She sucked in a deep breath of the still humid night time air of Las Vegas as she stole a glance at Brad. He was gorgeous, but could she go through will a one-night stand?

Sure part of her practically screamed or better yet begged for her to do it. But the rational part of her mind cautioned her. She didn't even know this guy. He could be a serial killer for all she knew. Suddenly overcome with anxiety she began to feel her heart rate increase as she noticed her hand was moving away from his. Maybe it was slowly sliding away from all the moisture that had made her hand damp with worry. Or maybe she was just subconsciously pulling her hand away?

It had been three years seen she'd been with a man. That's thirty-six months of celibacy. Granted none of the guys she'd dated were anywhere as gorgeous as Brad. He rated on a scale of one to ten, of one being butt-ugly, not even a blip on the radar to ten being Adonis-like quality. Brad came in at an impressive, eleven.

# Chapter 11

Brad must have sensed her resistance because he stopped just as the stepped up on the sidewalk directly across the parking lot across from the club and turned to face her. "I'm not some kind of killer or anything." He stated with the most sexiest grins she'd ever seen before, while trying to reassure her. She smiled at his admission and breathed a sigh of relieve, until her subconscious implore, "*would a killer really tell you though?*" She felt a new wave of panic wash over her as her eyes darted everywhere but the gorgeous man standing before her.

Before she could even think of an excuse to get out of this, he shifted closer to her. Rooted to the sidewalk, Haley stood stock still, eyes wide as she looked up into his mocha eyes that held her attention. His fingers plowed into her hair, as his palms cradling her head as he searched her eyes and slowly lowered his mouth to hers. His lips brushed across her a few times before he inclined his head and searched her eyes for permission to continue while keeping his hands in her hair. Feeling out of breath, like she'd just ran around the block a few times she gently nodded her head as she stared at his full lips. She licked her lips in anticipation. His body heat reached out and filled the space between them, caressing Haley's bare legs. He smelled like a unique blend of spices, citrus, and wood. It was irresistible. Something male and alluring, much like Brad.

Her hands ran along his wide shoulders to the back of his neck brining his lips to hers once again. She held on, as his slick tongue entered her mouth. He tasted like the beer he'd just drank, but mostly he tasted like a man. A man with sex on his mind. She liked the taste in her mouth. She liked the warm, powerful, possession of the kiss that flowed through her and warmed her all over.

Her toes curled inside her black pumps and her fingers dug into his thick dark hair. His hands never left her head. His mouth never left hers, yet she felt the kiss everywhere. His mouth devoured hers. Devouring all her rational thought. She hardly knew him, but she didn't dwell on that as he continued to feed her kisses that left her wanting more. More than just a panty combusting kiss. She moaned and leaned into him. "We better get out of here." He whispered against her mouth before pulling away from her.

"Why don't we go get something to eat." He suggested as he jerked his head in the direction of the restaurants lining the streets while he laced his fingers with hers. Haley nodded her head in agreement and the two casually strolled the streets ofVegas.

"So what do you do for a living?" Brad asked after he swallowed his bite of cheeseburger.

"I work as a nurse." Haley informed him as she pushed a French fry around her plate. Brad nodded his head enthusiastically as he took another bit of his burger.

"What kind of nurse?" He inquired after he took a drink of his soda.

"A labor and delivery nurse." She replied as she took a drink of her own soda. Since she finally put some food into her stomach, she didn't feel as tight headed as she did before. Which was a good thing. She'd hate to be a complete air head in Brad's presences.

"So, what do you do for a living?" Brad used his napkin and wiped his mouth clean, before answering. She couldn't help but stare at the at his mouth. He had the most perfect cupid's bow she ever seen. She had a burning desire, an aching need, for another kiss. He must have caught her ogling the perfection before her, because he deliberately and seductively slide the tip of his tongue his along his lower lip. The sexy gesture created a tingling sensation in the pit of her stomach. She gave a coy smile and nervously brushed her wayward hair behind her ear, before she shyly adverted her gaze to a neutral area. The table. Her eyes scanned the red and white blocks that lined the table.

"I work as a mechanic." The sound of his of deep, sexy voice had her lifting her head. Just as she did she witnessed the sexy grin curving up his mouth. She noticed he was watching her intently. She had to fight the overwhelming need to climb across the table and demand some more of his slow, drugging kisses.

What was wrong with her?

She'd been around guys before. None as gorgeous as Brad, but still this wasn't the first time she was having a conservation with the opposite sex.

Why was she such as nervous wreck?

*Because you want to jump his bones,* her subconscious implored.

Normally, her subconscious and herself were at war with each other, but right now she couldn't agree more. But, was she willing to put herself on the line, to make herself vulnerable, only to possibly face rejection? She knew for sure that her already suffering ego couldn't take another blow of refusal.

She needed to do herself a favor. She needed to get away from him, before she embarrassed herself. Sure, he might find himself attracted to her now. That was only from the alcohol fueling his desire for her. No man would ever find her desirable. Adam drove home that notion every time he'd either see her with someone or found out she'd been dating someone. He told her more than once she wasn't good enough for anybody. That she was only good at one thing. Being a mother. He also threw in with his snide remarks, that maybe with some practice, she might become better at something else too.

She didn't have to ask what he was talking about. She might be naive sometimes, but she wasn't stupid. As tempting as he was, she couldn't handle him dismissing her.

She needed something stronger to drink than what the fifties-themed dinner was offering.

She slowly inclined her head and risked taking another glance at Brad. His sexy smile made her heart turn over in response.

Yup! She needed to get way before the undercurrent of her desire for him, pulled her out to the sea of yearning, only to have a heavy wave of rejection come crashing down on her, and leave her clinging to a life raft of heart ache.

She started out by clearing her throat. "Well, I should be going." His sexy grin quickly vanished, only to be replaced with a forlorn expression. She quickly looked down at her hands that were twisting the material of her dress.

"Are you feeling any better?" The concern in his voice almost had her reconsidered her prior thinking. Almost. She just couldn't deal with his rejection.

"Yeah. I'm feeling much better. Thank-you." She kindly informed him as she slowly rose from her chair. "I'm just really tired."

"Well, then." Brad started out as he too rose from his chair. "Allow me to walk you back to the hotel."

"You don't have to do that. Stay. Enjoy yourself." She said, gesturing around the restaurant.

"Haley. It's dark outside." He informed her as he indicated out the window. Haley turned to look out the window he motioned to. "I-I'll just call a cab." She stammered nervously as she waved off his concern.

"Nonsense." He countered as he snatched the bill off the table and gestured for her to walk before him. He guided her over to the counter, that way he could settle the bill. His hand rested on the small of her back as they approached the counter. The warmth of his hand seeping into the thin material of her dress had her heart jolting and her pulse pounding.

A short blond haired woman that didn't look to be over the age of twelve, greeted Haley kindly. Haley's smile soon faded as the blond eyed Brad appreciatively. Her bright red lips curled up into a flirty smile as she coyishly batted her eyelashes at him.

Oh barf! Haley daftly thought as she suppressed the urge to roll her eyes. Brad removed his hand from her back to pull his wallet from his back pocket and handed the awe-struck woman his card.

The woman gingerly swiped his card through the machine before continuing to ogle him.

It was pathetic. Didn't this little hussy once think that maybe Brad and her where together? Apparently not as she continued to flirt with him.

"I'm sorry, Mr. Tyson. I have to scan your card again. I don't know what's wrong with the machine tonight?" Her child-like voice was grating on Haley's nerves. No one should be able to flirt with him, expect for her.

What the hell? She idly thought as she adverted her eyes to the floor and aimlessly searched for explanation as she felt herself tense up. Where in the hell did possessive thought come from.

Brad must have felt her become rigid. "Are you alright?" He whispered into her hair. His amused tone had her looking up at him. Enjoyment twinkled in the depths of his dark eyes.

Yeah. Good question. Was she alright? Just moments ago she wanted to get as far away from him as possible, now she wanted claw the overly friendly hostess's eyes out for flirting with him.

She needed to get a hold of herself and put as much distance as she could between Brad and herself. When she was near him, her senses reeled as if short-circuited.

"Yeah. I'm fine." Haley retorted quickly, too quickly. "I'm just going to go outside and call a cab." She said as she gestured towards the door. "Thanks again, Brad." She called out over her shoulder as the hostess slide his card for the third time.

"Haley?" Brad called out in a fluster as she scurried out the door.

She shouldn't be walking alone at night on the streets of Vegas. She should be calling a cab. Her thoughts were so jumbled right now as her heels pounded on the sidewalk. Each hurried stride got her one step closer to the hotel, where she would be safe. Safe from the strange people she was walking past, but more importantly, she'd be safe from Brad.

Just the thought of Brad, the confusion laced in his voice echoed in her mind and made the corners of her eyes well up with unshed tears.

She'd made up her mind thought. As soon as she got back to hotel, she was going to either tell Tanya in person or by letter, that she was catching the next flight to go back home. She hoped Tanya was still out. She didn't have the energy right now to deal with Tanya in person. She was going to go back to her life of misery. So what, if she didn't love Adam? At least she knew Megan was safe. That's all that mattered

This was crazy, she idly thought as she stopped at the crosswalk, and pressed the silver button, summoning the crosswalk light to appear. Maybe she was the crazy one?

"Haley." She picked up her pace and ignored Brad's calls from the distance as the orange hand was replaced with a white one. Her heels clicked on the pavement as she hurried across the walkway.

The sound of approaching, pounding footsteps from behind her suddenly sent a buzz of alarm signals to sound in her mind. Maybe she should've awaited for Brad to walk her back. Maybe she overreacted to the hostess's advances to Brad? Maybe she was just losing it.

She felt a hot tear streak down her cheek as she rounded the corner and slammed into a wall of muscles. She muttered some kind of an apology as she kept her eyes adverted and tired to step around the man that she plowed into. When a large hand wrapped around her arm, halting her movements, she quickly looked up through heavy lashes into concerned mocha eyes.

"Why didn't you wait for me?" Brad quietly asked as his hands cradled her head while the pads of his thumbs wiped the tears away. Haley tried to shake his hold, but he wouldn't relent.

Haley sighed defeatedly. "I'm just tired. That's all." She gave a coy smile. Brad squinted his eyes and cocked his head, like he wasn't believing her.

"Are you sure?" He harshly whispered as he lowered his head towards hers.

All she could do was nod her head as she watched his mouth. She wanted to feel his lips pressed against hers again. "I have a comfy bed you can lay in." He sweetly offered as his lips hovered against hers.

She knew if she took him up on his offer, she won't be sleeping in his bed. Not for a while that is. But, she couldn't do this. She managed to free herself from his embrace and placed a cautious hand against his chest. "Brad." She started out through a sigh. "I can't do this." She solemnly shook her head as she gauged his reaction.

"Do what?" He asked as his dark brows knitted together.

"This." She gestured her finger between the both of them. "I'm not that kind of girl."

"I never thought of you like that. I like you Haley." The sincerity in his voice made her want to laugh in his face. He slowly removed her hand from his chest and placed her palm on his side as he stepped closer to her.

She scoffed. "No you don't." She voice broke as she tried to move away from him, but he tightened his hold on her. Not that he was hurting her, but pressing her against him.

"I know you like me too, especially when I do this." Without notice his lips were on hers. She pressed her lips together, fighting the attempt to surrender to him, as his demanding lips caressed hers. His tongue traced the seam of her lips. "Don't fight Haley. Just go with it." He whispered against her mouth. Her attempts shattered with the hunger of his kisses. The caress of his lips against hers set her aflame. She knew playing with fire, she'd only get burnt, but none of that seemed to matter right now. She turned the heat up and created an inferno when she reciprocated. He smothered her lips with a demanding mastery as she threaded her fingers through his thick hair.

She felt the scratchiness of the building they were standing next to against her bare shoulders as he wedged her between it and him. He showered her with kisses on her mouth, along her jaw and down her neck. His kisses where define ecstasy as she tilted her head to the side, giving him better access as her eyes fluttered closed. She balanced herself on one leg as he lifted her other leg to his waist and slide his hand up her dress, caressing the back of her thigh.

The sounds of blaring horns and whistles, had Haley breaking t he kiss as she nervously looked down at his chest. Brad slowly removing his hand from under her dress while she placed her other foot on the ground.

"We better get out of here." He suddenly announced as he placed a kiss on top of her forehead. She smoothed down her dress before she laced her fingers with his offered hand. Maybe she'd regret her impulsive decision in the morning, but she'd dwell on it then. For now she was going to create blissful memories with a man she hardly knew, to keep her entertained on the lonely, boring nights a head of her.

# Chapter 12

The sound of someone clearing their throat made Haley pulling her lips any from Brad's. He grumbled as she slowly scanned the empty elevator. Her cheeks flushed as she quickly adverted her eyes to the floor as she traced her finger around her swollen lips.

"I guess this is our floor." Brad said as he extended his arm, gesturing for her to step out of the elevator first. Haley was the first to walk past the older man that appeared to be blushing also.

The soft click of her hotel room door shutting, had her heart drumming in her ears, as a flutter of nerves swirled in her stomach. Could she really go through with this? Sure, Brad was the most gorgeous man she'd ever encountered, and any girl wouldn't think twice about having a one-night stand with him. But was she really *that* kind of girl?

Guess so? Her lust-hazed mind thought as she pushed him up against the door and yanked his shirt wide open, revealing his tan, sculptured chest. The little blue buttons that closed his shirt were now scattered across the floor. She slide her palms along the warm, shimmering mountain of muscle and flesh. The tips of her fingers lazily traced the image of sharp teeth of a dragon just above the flat brown disc on his solid right pectoral. Her finger then trailed the red and black tints of scales along his collar bone to the hues of red and black diamond's deep-set into its hide on his shoulder. Then down his sides, abdomen and back. His whispered something against her throat.

She let out a startled squeal as he quickly spun her around and pinned her to the door. His mouth claimed hers, turning the kiss into a dance and duel of wet tongues and hot mouths. He slipped the pads of his finger tips under the edge of her dress and pressed his warm palm into the back of her thigh, holding her against his rock-hard shaft.

His fingers continued to glide up and down her bare thigh, his touch light and soft, making her shiver and moan deep in her throat.

Liquid lust rushed through her veins, combining with the mixed up and confused feelings deep in her soul.

The last ounce of her self-control faded away as Brad rubbed against her and his hands slid all over her body, touching everywhere, turning up the heat and taking over her control. Before she knew quite how it happened, he was pushing the thin straps of her dress down her shoulder. The silky black dress slide down her body with ease and pooled at her feet. She was just in her bra and panties.

Brad took a step back. His hooded eyes flared, momentarily in surprise. He gaze moved from her eyes, down her neck, to her shoulders, and ended at her breasts, with a pleased look.

His harsh breathing heaved his chest, as if he'd been jogging for ten miles. Haley knew the feeling.

"God, I love a woman in silk." His voice hoarse and deep as he lifted his hand and traced the scalloped edge of lace that cradled the swells of her breasts. "You're so beautiful. You make me forget."

Haley ran her tongue along her lips, while attempting to control her breathing. "Forget what?"

He glanced at her, then returned his attention to her nipples, which were two distinct pebbles in her pink bra.

"That I should take things slow. That I don't want to rush things and scare you away," he answered, even as he pressed his palms to her full breast. "But it's been a long time." Heat from his palms soaked through the thin material, and he pushed her breasts together, and kissed her deep cleavage.

"Why do you have to look this good?" His warm breath feathered across the swells of her breasts. "This would be so much easier if you weren't so damn attractive. If I didn't want you so much, that all I can think of is getting you naked," he growled.

Haley knew the feeling, all too well.

He lifted his face to hers and gave her a kiss that she felt clear to the soles of her block heels. He ran his hands down to the backs of her thighs and lifted.

She didn't hesitate to wrap her legs around his muscular waist. Her hands twisted in his hair as she trailed kisses down his thick neck with her eyes closed. He carried her across the room and gently laid her down. The coolness of the bedspread caressed Haley's sensitized skin. Street light filtered in through the curtains, casting long narrow stripes of muted light across Brad's face, as she ran her hand along the grow of stubble that coated his face.

He unhooked her bra and trailed fiery kisses to the side of her neck just above her clavicle, as she threaded her fingers in his hair.

She felt his breath warming the graceful swells of her breasts and her nipples hardened in response. At the same time she begun to grow more and more slippery and begun to unconsciously roll her hips, grinding against him. The ache in her stomach intensified as he fastened his mouth to one nipple and rolled the other between his thumb and pointer finger.

She wrapped her legs around his waist, guiding him closer. He ground his incredibly hard erection into her through the thin fabric of her panties driving her towards the edge until she knew she'd either stop or embarrass herself. Brad quickly stood from the bed and buttoned his pants, shoving them down his legs as fast as he could. When he stood back up, she gasped as his hard thick shaft shifted against his movements.

That monstrous thing was suppose to go where? She didn't dwell on it further as he climbed back on the bed.

He slowly trailed his lips away from her hardened nipple before sitting up on his hunches, looking down at her through hooded eyes. His finger teasingly trailed down her stomach, over her navel and brushed the top of her panties. Her body played along with his movements like a fine tuned instrument. Her back bowed of the bed once his lips followed the same path his fingers trailed. He gently eased her panties off of her as his placed hungry kisses along the inside of the thighs. Her fingers curled into his hair as he flicked her nub with his tongue, earning a soft moan from her. He teased her core with his finger, before he finally pushed through. Liquid warmth coated his finger as he worked another finger inside her of, stretching her. The only noises in the semi-dark room was her heavy breaths, and the sound of her arousal. Her warm sheath began to tighten around his finger as her hips moved to their own accord.

Nuh-huh.

There was no way she was going to cum until he was buried deep inside of her. He wanted to feel her clench around him, not his finger. For the first time that is. She muttered something as he withdrew his fingers. Before she could say anything else that might have made any sense to him, he captured her lips in a hungry kiss as he wrapped his arms around her back, pulling her to him.

Once she was on her knees, he moved behind her and rested his spread legs behind her as he snaked his arm around her stomach and slowly pulled her against him. "You want me, and I want to fuck you until you can't walk for a week," he said as he reached his hand between her parted legs and stroked her wetness. "Until you can't move. Can't think. Can't do anything, but scream my name. Do you want that, Haley?," he harshly whispered

He felt her tremble. He wasn't sure if it was from his words or his movements. All she could manage was a breathy, "Yes."

She was hesitant at first as she braced her one hand on the mattress and the other on his leg. He could feel how tense she was.

"I'm going to make it good. I promise." He hoarsely whispered against her neck between kisses. He started to feel her relax as she moved into him.

Her heart was hammering out of her chest and she felt so exposed like this. She'd never had sex from behind before, ever. She was ready to hop off the bed, grabbing her clothes and making a run for it before he whispered into her ear of his erotic promise. She didn't know if it was possible, but she felt herself becoming more aroused from his words. She began to relax and moved into him. His one arm snaked around her stomach as the other one gripped her hip pulling her into him. This was weird. She felt like she was going to sit on his lap, when she suddenly felt the tip of his erection brush against her.

Oh! God! It had be a long time since she felt this intimate as she slowly seated herself between his spread legs. She gasped as more of him entered her. "Easy baby." He whispered into her ear as she felt him shifting his hips around. "Oh! God!" She moaned softly as her head lulled to the side, her eyes fluttered closed and her grip on his forearm tightened. If he kept grinding against her, she was liable to set some kind of record.

They both groaned as she rested on his lap. She felt full, too full. But she wasn't going to let that stop her. She started to swirled her hips and cried out loud at the fullness. "Easy baby. There's no rush." He whispered against her neck as he continued to kiss her and palm her breast with both hands. When she felt comfortable enough with his girth, she rocked her hips against him. The stinging sensation was gone and was replaced with a hot, carnal need. "I'm going to move now." He informed her in a seductive voice. She was too aroused to form a coherent sentence, so she just nodded her head. He thrusts started out slow and even. She bucked against him. She didn't want slow. He must have figured out what she wanted. "Is this what you want?" His harsh voice was filled with lust as whispered against her ear while thrusting harder into her causing her to cry out. Both his hands dropped to her hips to steady her, as did hers, her fingers wrapped around his forearms.

She all she could do was nodded her head as his thrusting became harder and uneven. She could feel her insides begun to tighten. Brad must have felt it too, because his one hand gripped her hip and the other pressed against swollen clit. She wrapped both her hands around his neck clenched her fingers in his hair as she felt herself clench around his hard shaft. "Oh . . . God! . . . Oh . . . Brad!" She screamed as her climax ripped through her. She felt his shaft swell before he buried face against the crook of her neck and growled as he stiffened followed by three quick, thrust. As the spasms lessoned, Brad rolled to his side, breaking their precious contact as he took Haley with him. She burrowed herself into the curve of his body as she felt exhaustion suddenly wash over her.

# Chapter 13

Haley tried to slowly roll from her side, but something stopped her from rolling to her back. She picked her head up only to lower it back down to the pillow, she whimpered as her hand cupped her throbbing forehead.

Hang over's sucked. She idly thought as she squeezed her already closed eyes tight. Did she really drink that much last night? She tried to remember just how many drinks she had, but she couldn't concentrate with the loud snoring.

Snoring!?

She quickly forced her eyes open and willed the room not to spin as she slowly sat up. Her hair was like a veil covering her face. She brushed it back as she looked to the left of her and seen—Was that Brad? Lying in her bed naked?

Oh. God. She thought it was a dream. A dream that she slept with him. Various images from the night before decided at that moment to play inside her head, like giant, annoying slideshow. It felt that there was more to this so called dream but she couldn't wrap her mind around anything. Her head protesting from all the alcohol she'd consumed the night before. The further she sat up, the more the covers slipped off her naked body, further proving it wasn't a dream. "Oh. God." She mumbled to herself as she looked over his tanned, muscled back. Another tattoo of what looked liked barred wire wrapped around his thick bi-cep.

She rubbed her hands across her face, trying to wake-up or clear her mind, she wasn't sure which one. When something brushed against her left cheek making her pulling her hands away from her face.

"What the hell?" She grumbled as she examined her left hand out if front of her. She squinted against the throbbing as she stared at her hand. Was that? . . . was that? . . . a ring?

Deep mumbling caught her attention as she looked over towards Brad as he pushed himself up on his side.

Leaning his right elbow into the mattress, he ran his left hand through his disheveled hair revealing a ring, identical to hers.

"Oh. God!" She shrieked as she threw her hands over her mouth. She wasn't dream. Was she? She winced at her pitch. Nope. Not a dream. This was so not helping her throbbing head. She stared at Brad through wide, alarming eyes. "What?" His voice rumbled as he squinted against the sunlight that passed through the curtain in her room.

"Look!" She stabbed an accusing finger towards his hand as her other hand tried salvaging what was left of her modestly by clutching the sheets over her naked body. Brad stretched out his thick hand in front of him and blinked away the sleep a few times before focusing his attention to the ring on his left hand.

She couldn't read his expression to know what he was thinking, but if the sexy grin that was curving up his mouth was any indication, he wasn't having the same reaction that she was.

"Well, good morning. Wife."

"Wife!" She shrieked, making him wince for the second time in less than twenty minutes as she ripped the sheet from him and wrapped herself in it while she began pacing back and forth the bed as she nibbled her bottom lip. She looked frantic.

She absently looked down at the floor as her pacing increased, but she looked sexy as could be. Her tousled chestnut hair cascading carelessly down her tanned shoulders and back. When she looked down at him a few moments ago with those wide green terrified eyes, he just wanted nothing more than to hold her. She looked so terrified.

"There's no way we can be married." She informed him as she wildly flailed her hands around her as she continued to pace the floor. He wasn't sure if she was talking to him or to herself, since she still refused to look at him. He threw his legs over the side of the bed that she was pacing and reached out to her.

"We have to get this annulled." She quickly demanded.

Annulled? No freaking way.

He wasn't sure if she would move from him or not. She surprised the hell out of him when she went to him. He wrapped his arms around her hips and looked up at her.

"You don't want to be married?" He kept his voice even. He should be the one pacing the floor. He wasn't ready for marriage and all the other bullshit that went along with it. But for some reason being married to Haley didn't seem to scare the shit out of him. He could actually see himself growing old with her. Maybe he was still to hung over to be thinking clearly? But he already knew that he didn't want to loss her.

"It's not that I don't want to be married." She paused as she absently looked around the room again before bringing her attention back to him. "I've always dreamt of getting married." When she looked back down at him again, her beautiful emerald eyes were filled with unshed tears.

Brad took that moment to stand up. He didn't care if he was naked or not, or if she got offended with the hard-on that was poking her. There was one thing that he couldn't stand the sight of, was a woman crying.

"Shh. It's okay." He tried to reassure her as he pulled her into his arms and gently rubbed her back. The palm of one of his hands stroked her back in small circular motions, while the other hand cradled the back of her head. He placed a kiss on top of her head, as tired to make sense of why she didn't want to be married. Then it hit him. A lot of woman dream about their special day and put a lot of planning into it. Their wedding was spur of the moment. That had to be it.

She placed her small palms against his chest a few moments later, pushing herself away from him. He moved his hands to her hips, holding her close. "No. It's not okay." She whispered as she solemnly shook her head while staring down at his chest. "Why?" He asked in concern. Was she already married? He didn't remember seeing any rings, but then again he wasn't exactly checking out her hands last night or this morning either.

She slowly inclined her head to look up at him. Her bottom lip quivering. "Because. I'm already engaged." Her last word came out in a muffled howl as she buried her face into his chest as she continued to cry. Brad's hands stopped moving on her back as everything in him stilled.

*All ready engaged?* What the fuck?

"But, you're not even wearing a ring." Haley felt Brad's muscled chest stiffen from her admission. Not that she could blame him. It's not every day that a husband learns that his wife is already engaged to marry another man.

*Husband?* Ah! God! She couldn't believe she was actually saying that word in her mind. Sure, she always dreamt of being married, but in those dreams she was in love with that person. She was definitely not in love with Adam, but it was simple. She'd either marry Adam or risk loss her daughter.

"I never wanted a ring from him." Haley hoped that her answer pleased him enough to not warrant any more about this.

"Why?"

She should've known better, she thought dryly.

She didn't know Brad. Okay. She knew him better than she knew him last night, but still that wasn't enough to start a life together, but she guessed it would be for the best to let him know why she couldn't stay married to him. But first, she needed to get dressed.

"Let me get dressed first, then I'll tell you everything." She somberly said. Brad nodded his head in agreeance

She wondered what was his last name? Or more like what was her last name now? Oh! This was ridiculous she idly thought as she quickly shook that thought away as she zipped her jeans before opening the bathroom door and entering the bedroom. She couldn't be married to Brad. She was marrying Adam in a few more depressing weeks. But she wondered who's idea it was to get married in the first place? I couldn't have been hers. Could it have?

She hoped he remembered.

Maybe her admission was a good thing. Right? Maybe he didn't want to be married to her either? Maybe he'd realize the huge mistake for what it was?

A mistake? When she came out of the bathroom, she looked towards the empty, unmade bed. The prove of their love making was evident by the way the sheet were all rumpled. She felt her cheeks warm at the mere memory. But where was Brad?

Maybe he was in the kitchenette? The thick carpet silenced her movements as rounded the corner, and peeked around the doorframe. Empty.

Looking around the empty room suddenly sent an odd twinge of disappointment through her. She should be happy that he left. Right? But for some reason she wasn't. She was pulled from her miserable thought a few moments later by light knocking at the door.

Did Tanya forget her room card. Tanya? Oh shit! She was going to freak out if she caught wind of what happened last night. Not that Tanya wanted her to marry Adam. No! Just the opposite. She wanted to have Haley's head examined the day she told her about their unblissful day. She opened the opened the door and looked into forlorn mocha eyes that sent another twinge of disappointment through her.

So much for her theory, she thought dryly. Brad leaned against the door frame as he held onto two Styrofoam cup and a brown paper bag was tucked along his arm and side. "I didn't know if you were hungry." A sexy grin crept up his mouth making her mouth go dry.

*Why couldn't see stay married to him again?* Oh! Right! Adam! He looked even sexier than he did the night before. This was so not fair! His dark hair looked as if he ran his hand through it. A shadow of dark stubble coated his tanned face. His dark eyes twinkled. His thick bicep strained against his black t-shirt, and those snug, worn Levi's clung to him. And he was so her husband, if only for a couple hours anyways.

Haley gestured for him to come inside the room. When he walked past her she was greeted by the faint smell of his cologne. So not fair! She mumbled to herself, or so she thought. "What did you say?" He asked over his shoulder through a chuckle. "Nothing." She said quickly, too quickly.

# Chapter 14

After Haley and Brad finished their breakfast from the bakery he stopped at across the street, Haley had the painstaking task of letting Brad know why they couldn't stay married. During the course of their meal, they made small talk. She discovered that he lived in Minnesota as well. When she asked where in Minnesota, she about choked on her blueberry muffin.

Prick Pine, Minnesota wasn't a big town by any standards. If you sneezed while driving through . . . well sorry about your luck. Better luck next time. Turns out he lived on the same street as her.

What are the odds? He moved in there a year and a half ago. Shows how much she pays attention.

"Do you remember anything about last night?" There was a curious edge to his tone as he sat on the sofa, his elbows resting against his thighs as he hands dangled between his parted legs.

Haley looked over her shoulder towards him, and gave a coy smile before she licked her suddenly dry lips. "I remember being at the diner with you, and then coming back here together." She felt her cheeks flame as she shifted uncomfortable on the sofa next to him.

He gave her a mischievous grin and then cleared his throat before he continued. "Do you remember anything else?"

"Such as?" She wasn't going to play this game where she'd embarrass herself any further.

"When we left the hotel room."

"We left the room?" She asked in a disbelieving tone as her eyebrows drew together. As she turned to face him, the events of last night suddenly began to assail her. She did remember leaving the room with him. She did remember going to the 24-hour chapel and she did remember marrying him. She felt her stomach roll as a wave of nausea threatened to overcome her.

“Oh god! What about Megan?” She said in a panic, as her eyes searched aimlessly around the room. If Adam found out about this, she’d loss—

“Who’s Megan?”

When she told him she had a daughter, he couldn’t wait to see pictures of her. See was a little creped out at first, after all she didn’t really know him. Until she learned that he had all nephews and finally having a little girl in the family would be something new for his mother to fuss over. He stopped himself after he said that she would be spoiled rotten.

A twist of guilt knotted in her stomach. Haley felt bad for him, like she was taking something away from him, but she couldn’t loss Megan. Megan was her world. “When I refused Adam’s second proposal, he threatened me.” She looked down at the floor while she whipped away the tears that began to trail down her face. She looked over to him, her eyes darkening with pain.

“What did he threaten you with?” He promoted.

“There was this one time when Megan was three, she was burnt pretty bad when she was suppose to be watched by the sitter.” She stopped long enough to wipe her nose with a tissue before adding it to the mound that was heaped in the center of the coffee table. “She was in the hospital for three weeks." Her voice began to trail off before she finished what she was saying. "Those were the worst days of my life." Her whispered words were so broken as she spoke. Before Brad could wrap his arms around her to comfort her, she lunged herself into him and held onto him tightly. He gently stroked her back as he felt her trembling as the soft sobs escaped her.

He clenched his jaw to the point that he felt pain. He didn't even know this Adam guy and he already wanted to kill him. She pulled away from him, clearing her throat while brushing her hair behind her ears and sniffled a few times before she spoke. "Somehow Adam found out about it and used it to his benefit. He told me that if I didn't marry him, than he turn me into child welfare for being an unfit mother."

"Why would he force you to marry him though?" She scoffed as she traced the tips of her fingers below her eyes, capturing the remaining tears before looking at him. Hurt and anguish lay naked in her emerald eyes. "He's running for Governor and in order to be a 'convincing' man, he has to appear to be a family man." He felt numb with increasing rage and shock. For someone to use his own child to his advantage was just an asshole. "But you said it was an accident? Right?" He sounded unsure, even to his own ears. But it wasn't making any sense to him.

She let out a heavy, frustrated sigh. "Adam has a lot of clout. He told me he could very easily make it look as if I'd intentionally harmed my own child."

What the hell kind of jackass did that? Then it dawned on him. Adam was in politics after all. He hadn't meet a single one of them that wasn't corrupt.

She looked over to Brad and jutted her chin towards the damp spot on his shirt. "Sorry," she said sheepishly as she clasped both of her hands on her lap and adverted her eyes to the floor.

"There nothing to be sorry about." He placed two fingers under her chin. Once he knew her eyes would be level with his he coaxed her face towards his with the same two fingers still tucked under chin.

"I'm so sorry for everything. Sorry for not being able to give you the live you deserve. Sorry for—" He scooted closer to her and placed his finger on her quivering lips, silencing her. "Enough. You have nothing to be sorry for," He whispered, cupping her face in his hands and gently used the pads of his thumbs to brush away her tears. "It's not your fault that those bad things happened to Megan. You trusted the sitter to look out for her while you provided for her." She tried to defiantly shake her head, like she didn't believe a word he just said. She opened her mouth to say something else, something that this Adam asshole probably brain washed into her head, when he silenced her again. This time it was with his mouth.

He felt her resistance at first until we ran his tongue along the slit of her lips. Her fingers curled into his hair as she welcomed his tongue into her mouth. The kiss grew hungry as he pressed her into the couch. As her back touched the couch she moaned into his mouth. His hand slipped under her shirt and caressed her smooth soft skin along her stomach as she clawed at the back of his shirt, trying to pull it off. Brad broke their kiss long enough to rid himself of his shirt and then pressed himself against her again. He hands made quick work of unbuttoning her jeans and releasing her zipper. Just as his hand was slipping inside her panties, to the wetness that he knew awaited him, the hotel room door swung open.

"Haley?" A female voice called out. Before Brad could pull his hand out of her panties, the band on his watch got stuck on the metal tab of her jeans. "Hal—Oh! My! Don't let me interrupt." Said the woman standing in the door way with her hand shielding her slight as she pushed the door closed.

"Tanya." Haley called out to her friend as he finally freed his watch. "You can come back in the room now." Haley called out over her shoulder towards the direction of her friend's retreating back. Brad pulled his shirt back on as

Haley adjusted her bra before sitting up on the couch next to him.

"I should get going." He said before glancing at his watch. Haley nodded her head as she walked him over to the door. He raised his hand to brush her hair behind her ear. "Don't worry. We'll get through this together." She leaned her head into his hand as she nodded again as he bent down and captured her lips for a quick kiss.

As he reached inside his pants pocket to retrieve his key card, he leaned his head against the closed door. Why was he giving her false hope? He didn't know what he was up against. All he knew so far was this Adam guy was blackmailing Haley. Using her daughter against her to get what he wanted. The same thing Brad wanted, just for different reasons. There had to be something he could do for her. As he slid the key making a little green light appear, a thought suddenly occurred to him. He slammed the door shut in a hurry as he sprinted across the room in search of his cell phone. As he waited for the call to connect, he prayed his idea would work.

"Hello, Mrs. Tyson." Tanya whispered through a giggle as she moved alongside Haley making her way to her locker. Haley's head snapped up and quickly looked around, making sure no one heard her. When she didn't see anyone, she turned her attention to Tanya with a lethal glare. "Shh!" She hissed as she gestured with her pointer finger against her mouth as her eyebrows drew together. "I don't want anybody knowing." She hissed as she continued to look around.

Yup. She was paranoid. And with good reason too. If Adam heard about this, she couldn't imagine what he would do. It's not that she was worried about Adam causing Brad physical harm . . . No! Just the opposite. Brad could very easily beat the shit out of Adam. No she was worried—

"I don't know why you're hiding him." Tanya started out as she opened her locker. "If I had a husband that looked like him, I'd be letting every bitch know he's mine." Tanya said as she paused to wave her hand in from front her, like she was trying to cool herself down. Haley knew the feeling.

"You know why I haven't said anything." She spat out. She didn't mean to sound so bitter, but she couldn't help it. There was a lot at stake here.

"I know. I know." Tanya said in a sympathetic tone. "I'm sorry." She gave an impish smile as she shrugged her shoulders before returning her attention to her locker.

Great! Now she felt like an ass for hurting her friend's feelings. She really hated Adam Lucas.

"How was your trip girls?" Wendy, the other OB/GYN nurse asked with enthusiasm as Tanya and herself made their way to the nurse's station. "Did you bring anything good back?" Wendy inquired over her shoulder as she slide the cover closed to the charts she was done with and moved onto to the next chart. Tanya's sudden snort, that was quickly covered by spell of dry coughing after Haley nudged her in the ribs. Which only drew Wendy's unwanted attention their way. Her expectant smile widen as she looked from Tanya to herself. Tanya couldn't seem to help herself as she started snickering, making Wendy's eyebrow shot up in concern.

"Is she alright?" Wendy asked, frowning.

"She's fine." Haley reassured Wendy quickly as she patted Tanya's back while still looking into other woman bewildered blue eyes. "She just needs something to drink." Haley continued offhandedly. Wendy slowly nodded her head but she still had the look of doubt of her face, like she didn't believe Haley.

"She's right." Tanya whispered hoarsely between gasps as she clutched her throat. "I need something to drink." She cleared her throat. "My throat is dry." She quickly turned on her heel and practically ran to the vending machine, giggling the whole way.

*Traitor!*

Haley turned her attention to Wendy and gave a careless shrug, before sitting next to her and looking over the remaining charts. She had a feeling it was going to be a long night.

# Chapter 15

"Brad, phones for you." Informed Steve, the other mechanic as he hooked his thumb over his shoulder, gesturing towards the office. Brad stood up from his bent over position as he wiped his grease covered hand on a gray rag as he made his way over to the office. He rubbed at the back of his neck that had become stiff as he walked through the doorway. Changing the spark plugs on this car was really becoming a pain in his ass. Normally the job was a quick one, but not when the plugs had somehow fused themselves onto the engine block. Now he was a few hours behind with his other work, and that was probably Mrs. Henderson on the phone asking him again if he had her car ready.

"This is Brad." He said cradling the phone between his cheek and shoulder as he continued to wipe away the grease.

"Hi, honey. How was your trip?" His mother asked in a bright tone. A too brightly tone that had his dark eyebrow arching, suspiciously. He had an unsettling feeling in the pit of his stomach that she was up to something.

"Alright, I guess." He said not sounded sure of himself. He wasn't about to tell her, he got married. It's not that Haley didn't want anybody to know. It's the fact that his mom would through a royal fit if she found out her "baby" got married. He was twenty-seven years old and didn't think he fit that category anymore. But being since he was the youngest of three children.

"That's good, dear. Did you meet anyone?" She asked sounding hopeful.

Yes! Mom. As a matter of fact you now have a daughter-in-law. He thought dryly.

Ah, shit. He idly thought as he shoved his fingers through his hair and let out a frustrated sigh. Blind date, Kate was on the lurch again. That's what he and his friend's named his mom when she mentioned to random girls she'd met, that she had a single son.

She really needed to stop this shit. Just because his older brother's got married. Brandon, was divorced now, but still just because his brother's had settled down and gave grandchildren, now she expected him to do the same thing. Which, he kind of already did. But he couldn't tell her that. God! He hoped his sister could help them out. He hated not being able to tell anyone. He wanted the world to know she was his, without risking Megan.

He turned his head and looked over his shoulder out the glass window that separated the garage bays from the office and noted all other mechanics working, either under the hoods of cars or laying on creepers working underneath cars. No one was paying any attention to him.

"Ah, Mom. I really need to get back to work. The guys are looking for me. I'll talk—"

"I won't hold you up any longer than. Be here at seven." She informed him as she cut him off.

"I have plans." He sternly countered back.

"I'll see you at seven, and Bradley? This time try to be nice to the young lady." She warned, ignoring Brad's for mentioned plans. He hated when she called him that.

What? It wasn't his fault that he may have said something offending to the woman that his mother brought home, thinking she'd be perfect for Brad, causing the girl to run out of the house in tears. With a name like Ophelia, it was pretty hard to not say anything to her. At least he didn't ignore her like his did the others. Did his mother think of that? No!

"Fine," he said on an exasperated sigh. This was it though. He was going to sit his mother down and simply explain that she needed to stop being Blind date, Kate. But, he had a feeling it was going to be easier said than done.

Did her car just growl at her? Haley idly thought as she popped the hood to her car. A puff of gray smoke billowed out from underneath as she shoved the hood up. Coughing and fanning the offensive smell away, she aimlessly searched for the problem. It all looked confusing to her. What in the hell was all of this for anyway? With a careless shrug she reached for her cell phone and dialed for a tow truck.

Good thing she had the day off, she idly thought after the tow truck arrived and hour and a half later. It was bad enough that she had to go to a different garage. When she talked to Howie earlier, her first choice for car repairs he informed her that he was too busy to fit her car in this week, since his help up and left him, leaving him to all the work. He wouldn't be able to look at her car for probably another three weeks.

She couldn't be without a car for that long. Howie, suggested she take her car to the other garage in the next town. He reassured her they did good work when she was hesitant. Howie was after all a friend of the family and he never steered her wrong before.

Right now she didn't care where her car was dropped off at. As far as she was concerned the tow truck driver could leave her and her car in the Wal-Mart parking lot they were passing, and she'd figured the damn thing out for herself, just as long as his eyes didn't devour her anymore than they already had.

When she handed over her towing membership card, the sneaky bastard tried to look down her sweater that was poking through her unzipped coat. She made quick work and zipped her coat up to the point that the top of the coat dug into her chin. When he heard the telltale sound he cocked a suspicious eyebrow her way. She fringed an innocence expression when she sweetly informed him she was cold. She was glad it was cold out and she lived in Minnesota. Where one day it could be seventy degrees and the next thirty degrees. It was after all April.

Now, she sat inside the sweltering cab of the tow truck sweating profusely as the driver named Jay cranked the heat on high, in hopes she'd unzipped her coat. That so was not happening. She'd rather dehydrate than be visually groped.

As soon as she seen they were nearing the dilapidated garage, surrounded by a variety of cars, she stumbled out of the tow truck before the driver even removed her car from the bed, in search of something to drink. Along her search, to avoid dehydration she collided into a solid wall of a muscles from not paying attention to where she was heading.

She hurriedly unzipped her coat to cool down, only to be heated up again. She quickly looked up into deep mocha eyes that locked with hers. He put his hands on her shoulder to steady her. She began to fell woozy but didn't think it had anything to do with the fluids she'd lost earlier. The man that was holding onto her reignited the same spark that he'd lit a few weeks ago. She felt the warm tingling sensation growing between her legs again, as her stomach fluttered.

"What are you doing here? Is Megan okay?" His concerned deep, rich voice sounded thick with sleep even though he was wide awake, waiting for her to answer.

"Hmm? Yeah? Everything's fine" She said sounded distracted, which she was as she craned her neck to look at the front of the building again. She couldn't even see the name clearly. The white paint was chipping to the point that the only letters she could understand was the G and R. "I didn't know this is the garage you worked at." She replied, pleased at how nonchalant she sounded as she willed herself to relax.

"Is something wrong with your car?," He said as he walked alongside of her, clearly fighting the urge to wrap his arm around her. She so bad wanted to grab onto his hand.

"Yeah. It won't start and when I tried to start it after it shut off, it sounded like it growled at me." She informed him.

"It growled at you?" He asked in mock disbelief.

She raised her head to look up at him. When she seen his was looking down at her, she narrowed her eyes and tried her best to glare at him for mocking her. She failed as soon as he gave her his signature, impish grin. She felt her insides melt.

Since she was in another town? She didn't see the problem with it. Brad looked down at their entwined hands and then to her with a sexy, mischievous grin. A grin that made her stomach flutter as a pulsating sensation occurred between her legs.

"Don't worry. The guys will have your car running in no time." He assured her as they moved closer to the building

"Jerry!" Brad called out as he peeked his head inside on the garage bays.

"Yo!" A deep voice hollered back. Haley didn't see anybody move. "I'm taking a break." Brad said not waiting for a respond as he practically ran to his truck. Haley had a hard time keeping up with him.

"What are you doing?" She asked after he hopped inside the truck on the driver's side and closed the door. "Going to check under your hood." He stated with that same sexy grin on his face as he started the engine and backed the truck out of the parking lot. For some reason she didn't think he was talking about her car. "What about my car?" Haley asked with concern in her voice as she gestured towards the garage that was now behind them. "It's not going anywhere." He said matter-of-factly as turned his blinker on, signaling a left hand turn pulling into a dirt road.

"Where are we going?" She tried to hide the panic in her voice, but she felt like she was losing the battle.

“I plan on making love to my wife if you don’t mind.” His voice rumbled seductively as he throw the truck into park and turned the engine off. He grabbed her hand and pulled her closer to him. She freely slide across the seat. When her thigh rested against his, he still kept tugging on her hand until she straddled his lap.

“What if someone sees us?” She questioned as he kissed the side of her neck while his hands made quick work of pulling her shirt over her head.

“It just you and me baby.” He whispered against her neck. That’s all she needed to know as she ground her hips against him.

# Chapter 16

Her wrinkled toe broke through the white foam of bubbles as she pushed the brass knob with her big toe, turning the hot water on, warming her chilled off bath water.

What a day. She thought as she leaned her head back against the bath cushion, being careful not to push the hair clip securing her hair into her scalp, and closed her eyes enjoying the warmth that surrounded her. She worked a double shift today and her feet where killing her. Brad was coming over to her house tonight for supper, since Megan was staying at a friend's house for the night. They'd been back from Vegas for almost three weeks. In those three weeks, Brad came over to her house every night after

Megan was in bed, and he left every morning before she awoke.

She was still hesitant about introducing Megan to Brad. What if things didn't work out between herself and Brad? She didn't want Megan to be the one to suffer because of it. Megan already suffered enough at the hands of her father. She couldn't do that to her little girl.

But it was also crazy to be married to a man that didn't live under the same roof as her. Or when they were together, they had to seek around.

How long could Brad put up with this before he demanded a divorce?

After her bath she was going to dress in her flannel pajamas, drop a disc in the DVD player, and order a pizza for them. Normally she cooked, but since Megan was staying at a friend's house tonight she was opting for the easiest.

Tanya begged her to go out with her tonight, since she finally had a night off, but Haley flat out refused. The last time she went out drinking with Tanya, she wound up married. The last place she wanted to be was in a bar. She didn't want to meet some man and somehow married to him too. Granted, she wasn't in Vegas this time, but still.

No. Thank you. One husband and one fiancé was plenty enough to deal with.

She just settled on the couch when the door bell rang. She frowned at the door. That had to have been the quickest pizza ever made she idly thought as she moved towards the door. Maybe Brad forgot his key, but she hoped it was the pizza guy because she was starved. That was until she opened the door.

"Hi Haley." The rather annoying voice drew out. She inwardly cringed as she looked up into Adam's hazel eyes. What in the hell did he want? And more importantly, why was he here? Drunk? He never came to her house unless he called first.

Did he know about Brad? She suddenly felt her heart rate pick up the pace.

She didn't have a choice last week when she had to put up with him. He had Megan for the day. More like Judith had Megan for the day. Adam didn't give two shit's about his own flesh and blood unless he was in the public eye. Then he'd pretend to be the loving father. Pretending he was kissing her on the cheek, when the whole time he was threatening her to be a good girl and smile pretty for Daddy.

It was very pathetic and downright stomach churning.

But, now she did have a choice. Megan wasn't home. Depending on her mood, she might be civilized to him. Maybe? She didn't want to piss him off enough to make her life a living hell. Not that she wasn't currently living like that.

"What can I help you with, Adam?" Before the last syllable even touched her ears she was already regretting asking the question as a carnal smile slowly crept up his mouth.

"I'll show you what you can help him with." He informed in a drawn out husky tone as his pulled his hand from his pocket, moving it down to his crotch and cupped himself in a provocative gesture.

Okay. Scratch the 'civilized' part. Was he checking to see if his manhood was still there? Was he trying protecting himself? What? Because if he thought for one minute that she was going to touch him—She threw her head back and snorted out loud as she thought about that last part. Whoever said beggars can't be chooser obviously never came face-to-face with Adam before.

"Look, Adam—" She was getting ready to give him the brush off when he interrupted her by abruptly pinning her between himself and the doorframe as he pushed his rather hard erection into her hip. "I bet if you had this in you,"

He shoved more of himself onto her, stressing his point while he pressed her even harder into the frame, causing the wood to bit into her back and taking away her ability to take deep breath, "like you let your boyfriend do, you wouldn't be laughing. Would you?" His warm, alcohol laced breath feathered across her neck as he irritably hissed into her ear.

Normally she didn't feel threatened when a man innocently hit on her and she turned him down, but now she was reconsidering, and hoping for the damn pizza delivery guy to hurry the hell up.

"Get off of me!" Someone screamed from the distance. Brad's beer bottle hovered below his bottom lip as he turned to look at Evan's equally confused expression as the two sat on Brad's back porch. They both gave a careless shrug as Brad lifted his bottle to his lips and took a drink. It wasn't coming from his house, so he didn't care who—He stopped his pondering as his gaze moved around the deck. Where the hell was Keith? Did he go inside to take a leak? He looked to the closed back door. Nope. Did he leave and Brad didn't realize it? Nope. His blue pick-up truck was parked next to Brad's garage.

"Where's Keith?" Brad asked already having a pretty good idea.

"I don't know. I thought he left." Evan said as he continued to text from his cell phone.

"His trucks still here," Brad said pointing the bottle in his hand towards the garage.

"He's probably . . . . Ah, fuck." Brad bit out as he quickly got to his feet, tossing his beer bottle to the wooden deck and rushed down the steps, leading to his back yard. He pushed the wooden gate with such a force that one of the metal hinges snapped from the wooden post, leaving it dangling. Just as Brad and Evan rounded the corner of his house, they spotted Keith talking to some woman.

Who was screaming? Evan and him stormed over to Haley's house to see some man curled up on his side, his legs tucked up to his chin, mumbling incoherently. Brad clenched his fist and hauled ass towards her porch.

"Dude! That was awesome! You should've seen it. She kicked that guy in the balls." Announced the pizza delivery guy as he stared at Haley in awe. Brad felt a moment of pride in his wife.

"Yeah, yeah, yeah. Shows over. What do I owe you?" Brad grumbled. He was running out of patience. Brad paid the kid and then shoved him down the sidewalk. "Man, she's my hero." The kid babbled as he finally got into his car and drove away.

"You ever touch me again, and I promise you'll be tasting your balls next time!" Haley spat out as she straddled some guys hip, shaking with rage as her hands clenched into fist and whirling her arms around him like a dysfunctional fan blade. The man's arm were curled up around his head and neck, protecting himself from her wild swings. Brad's eyes widen at her announcement. He suddenly had the urge to cover himself.

"Remind me to never piss her off." Evan whispered from beside him.

"Someone help!" The man screamed but he made no attempt to move her. Smart man, Brad idly thought, while grinning as he and Evan climbed the step to her porch.

"Haley?" Brad said slowly as he approached her. He didn't want to frighten her and run the risk of her attacking him. But he had to get her off this guy, so he could kick his ass for touching his wife.

"Next time!" She ducked her head under Brad's arm and shouted her warning at the guy. "Do you hear me!? Adam!"

"He heard yo—" He replied with heavy irony as he looked down at the doorway, being careful of the step. That is until the name Adam registered into his mind. He slowly lifted his head and ominously turned to face Adam as his gaze narrowed, murderously. He felt Haley's shaking hand grab onto his shoulder. Her finger tips pressed into him as she tried to pull him towards her.

Not happening. His rage knew no boundaries as he jerked his shoulder from her grasp. When he expelled each breath he took, it sounded like he was growling.

"Brad!" Haley warned through a sob. "Don't do this," she pleaded in a desperate tone.

"Man. You don't want to do this." Evan's anxious tone made Brad looked towards him and then to the hand that Evan pressed against his chest, trying to stop him from going after Adam.

Yeah. Stopping him was like trying to stop a freight train with your hand. He turned his murderous glare at Evan and growled his warning, to back off. Evan's hands flew up in surrender as his eyebrows shot up his forehead. "Dude. You're on your own." Evan replied quickly, sounding defeated as he stepped away.

"What are you going to do? Hit me, big boy?" Adam taunted as he looked up to Brad. Adam's cocky tone had his fist clenching and unclenching. Brad closed the distance between them as he watched Adam slowly swallow. "Stay. The. Hell. Away. From. Her." He uttered harshly.

"You can't tell me what to do." Adam smugly countered as he jabbed his finger into Brad's chest. Brad slowly looked down at his finger and then back to Adam and gave him a warning glare. Adam quickly removed his finger before continuing, "She my fucking fiancée you dickhead. I'll touch her whenever I wan—"

Adam was suddenly cut off as Brad quickly slammed his back against the solid wooden porch beam as he wrapped his fingers against Adam's neck and squeezed. Adam hands desperately clawed at Brad's relentless hold.

"Stop it!" Haley screamed from the distance as choking sounds escaped Adam. The pleaded look in Adam's hazel eyes made a menacing grin curve Brad's upper lip. "You touch my wife again and I'll kill you." He bit out sharply between clenched teeth, before pulling his hand away from his throat.

Adam bent over resting his hand on his thighs as he coughed deeply a few times. Brad directed a warning glare at Adam's hunched body. His arms rigid with rage as he own chest heaved.

"You!" Adam drew out, snarling as he straightened his posture, pointing a reproachful finger at Haley while his other hand rubbed against his reddened neck as his chest continued to heave. "You can kiss your daughter good-bye."

A stomach wrenching scream abruptly pulled Brad's awareness from Adam's retreating back. He turned his raged attention to the source of the noise. His eyes flared momentarily as he felt his anger slipping away only to be replaced with regret. Haley dropped to her knees, her hand flung her out in simple despair towards Adam's fading back as she screamed.

Fuck! What had he just done?

"Haley, let me help you into the house." Brad tried pulling her to her feet, but she wouldn't budge. Adam was going to take her baby away.

"Haley, baby. Let me—" Haley quickly cut him off as she abruptly got to her feet, taking him by surprise and shoved him away. Or as best as she could. "Stop with the Haley baby crap." She shouted at him as she tried to move past him. He gently grabbed a hold of her arm, stopping her and turned around to face her. She twisted her arm trying to get out of is hold, but he wasn't letting go.

"Let me go!" She demanded through a sob, but he only pulled her closer. She didn't want to be closer to him. She didn't want to be held by him.

She needed to go get Megan. She needed to rock her little girl in her arms and never let her go. There was no way Adam was going to take her away from her. She'd flee the states if she had to.

She twisted in his arms as he held her closer to him. She closed her fist and begun to pounded on his chest as she screamed at him. "This is all your fault!" She continued to pound on his chest and scream until she exhausted herself and went sag against him. He held her close as wept loudly.

# Chapter 17

"This is really good, Mrs. Tyson." Haley happily informed Brad's mom as she took another bite of pot roast. Normally, she didn't like anything that was roasted because it was always too dry, but this was heavenly.

She was also trying to get on the woman's good side. Ever since Brad introduced her to his mother as his *friend*, which kind of hurt since she thought they were more than just friends, since the truth about their marriage was out in the open now. She hoped she hide her disappointment well, as she pasted on a fake smile. But his mother kept looking at her with an uneasiness expression. What the hell did she do?

Her own uneasiness towards Brad was slowly starting to fade away from the other night when he lost his temper and informed Adam of their marriage.

Brad stood by her side just like he said he was going to do. She even gave in and let him drive to pick Megan up that night from her friend's house. She was nervous at first. She hadn't brought any of the men she'd dated in the past around Megan. But Brad wasn't just some man she was dating. He was after all her husband. Megan instantly fell in love with him. The two were becoming inseparable. But wasn't there to love about Brad?

"I'm glad to like it dear. And please, call me Kate." She said with a pleasant smile as she sat at the head of the table with her own plate in front of her, untouched. Haley quickly scanned the table to see if anyone else was eating their food. Brenda, Brad's sister sat beside Haley with her hands clasped in her lap with a forlorn expression on her face. Haley noted she didn't touch her plate. It was the same way with Brad's nephew, Connor.

She didn't think she'd ever be able to thank Brenda enough. After some convincing, Brad finally persuaded her to talk to his sister about what Adam was forcing her to do, which just happens to be a lawyer. Brad made Brenda promise she wouldn't tell their mother about their marriage.

Not that he was ashamed of her. He just wanted to be the one to tell her in person.

Brenda agreed and the next day a harassment order had been filed against Adam. Brenda assured her that is order wasn't something permanent, but it would buy her some time and prolong their wedding. She felt a bottomless peace and satisfaction. If even only temporarily, she'd take it.

She looked over her shoulder towards Brad. When he seen her looking at him, he gave her a wink and squeezed her knee under the table. He was eating his food. What the hell was going—

Haley's pondering was quickly put on hold when she heard someone call out from the distance. "Hello?" All eyes turned towards the doorway leading into the living room.

"Where in here, Cal." Kate gleefully called out. Her fidgety thumb twirled around the sapphire ring on her finger. A nervous gesture, perhaps?

"Who the hell is Cal?" Brenda irefully demanded as she looked over towards her mother, with a wicked gleam in her eyes. "Oh, relax!" Kate scolded Brenda. "I invited someone over for your brother."

Haley's stomach twisted as Brad grumbled something as he pushed his plate away. "I'm sorry I'm running late." Cal said as she walked into the dining room and hung her black purse from the back of the chair.

"Oh, that's fine dear." Kate warmly said as she patted the woman's hand in a understanding gesture. "It's not easy being a lawyer, is it?" Kate said she picked up her fork and dug into her food, that was now cold.

A scoff from across the table made Kate turn her head and glare at her daughter.

"What?" Brenda demanded as she replaced her glass of water back down to the table. "You think *my* job isn't easy?" Brenda implored as she pushed a carrot around on her plate with her fork.

Kate cleared her throat as she wiped the corners of her mouth with her napkin. "I didn't say that dear. Besides, this isn't about you." She turned her head and smiled at Brad. "This is about your brother." She picked up her fork and begun finishing her meal.

Brad leaned his arm over Haley's chair, as Callie rambled on and on about stuff that Haley had absolutely no idea what any of it meant. His hand gently caressed her shoulder. She could feel the tension rolling off of him. Was he tensed because he didn't want this woman here anymore than she did? Or was he tense because he didn't know how he was going to tell his mother about their marriage?

Callie abruptly ended her non-stop babbling as her eyes narrowed on Brad's hand caressing Haley's shoulder. Her piercing blue eyes searched Brad and then Haley. "Are you two together?" She asked with great interest. She looked at them expectantly. Brad opened his mouth to say something, but she stopped him and informed Callie that yes. Yes they were. Callie quickly dropped her lashes to hide the hurt as Brad groaned.

Callie whipped her head up a few moments later, and pasted a fake smile on her face as she looked to Kate and shrugged her shoulders. "Well, this is awkward." Haley felt Brad tense from Callie's reply and apparently he gave her a warning glare. "What . . . what I . . . I meant to say was I didn't want anyone feeling awkward with my being here." She stammered her clarification.

"Why should it bother you if they are together? I think they make a cute couple." Brenda snidely informed Callie. Haley heard Kate's sharp intake of a stunned breath. "Bradley, why didn't you tell you where bringing someone with you." Kate demanded with a frown on her face as she tossed her napkin on the table.

"Well, mother. I wish I could say it was nice being here, but then I'd be lying. Come on Connor." Brenda said as she stood from the table and pushed her chair in.

What the hell just happened here? He found himself asking that question to himself more since he meet Haley. But more importantly, what the fuck was his mother thinking? He idly thought as he stared absently at Haley's untouched plate. He thought he made it perfectly clear to his mother that she was to stop interfering in his personal life after he was forced to meet Janet last week. Apparently not clear enough.

"Callie, dear. I'm so sorry you had to witness this. Things aren't usually this awkward?" His mother casually said with an apologetic smile on her face as she pushed her plate away.

"Awkward for whom, mother? You or Haley?" His words were loaded with ridicule.

"Bradley! Don't you talk to me like that!" Kate sternly warned him.

"Talk to you like the meddling mother that you are? How in the hell else am I suppose to talk to you?" His voice hardened.

"How was I suppose to know you were going to bring a girl here?" She gave a careless shrug.

"Exactly! How many girls have I brought home?"

"Well, none. But when you said she was your—" Her voice trailed off as she slumped back into her chair. "Oh dear lord." His mother drew out before covering her face with her hands, as Brad's words sunk in.

"Would someone mind telling me what's going on here?" Callie demanded as she looked from Brad to Kate.

Kate removed her hands from her face and pushed herself up in her chair. "Brad just brought his first girlfriend home." Kate stared out over the table in bewilderment.

"No mother. She not my girlfriend. She's my wife."

"You're married?!" Callie inquired incredulously as she regarded them with a mortified look, before she turned an accusing glare at Kate.

"Don't look at me that way." Kate defensively retorted to Callie, before she turned her attention to Brad. "Brad, why didn't you—?" Kate paused as her mouth hung open from Brad's response, while she ignored Callie's reproachful glare. His mother for once was speechless.

"Well this is a first." Brad said sarcastically as an impish smile curved his mouth as he as he looked over to Haley and laced his finger with her. "Why didn't I tell you before?" Brad asked finishing his mother's unspoken question. "Because I wanted to tell you in person."

"I don't know what kind of sick joke you people are playing here" Callie incredulously demanded, as she looked at Brad accusingly. "I want nothing to do with it." She hissed.

"Oh. You poor girl. You must think I hate you" Kate finally spoke before she dropped her head into her hands in despair.

"There no game. Just a meddling mother" Brad mockingly informed the seething woman as he brought Haley's hand up to his mouth an placed a kiss.

Callie quickly rose from the table as well, her hands resting on her generous hips. "I'm outta here"

Brad lifted his head from Haley hand to look at the madder than a junk yard dog, Callie. His face split into a wide mischievous grin. "See ya."

# Chapter 18

"Mom!"

"And look at this one." His mother gushed as she turned the page, further embarrassing him.

"Mom! I really don't think Haley wants to see the millions of pictures you have from when I took baths." Brad playfully warned his mom as he tried to snatch away the photo album.

Kate swatted Brad's hand away and repositioned the offensive album on her lap. "Nonsense Bradley. Besides, it's nothing she probably hasn't already seen." She informed Brad in that mothers-now-it-all voice. "After all, you're a married man now." Kate cooed as she her fingers cupped around the bottom of his chin and gently shook it.

"Mom!" Brad tried to sound outraged, but the grin that curved his mouth made that impossible as he moved from his mother's embrace. Haley tried to hide her smile by firmly pressing her lips together but a soft giggle escaped, making Brad's narrow at her. "Laugh now, woman!" He playfully warned making her laugh out loud.

"What? I know how the younger generation is. Don't forget I was your age and one time and your father and I—"

"Please don't paint any picture of you and dad in my head." Brad interrupted in disgust as he closed his eyes while rubbing his temples. She was glad Brad talked her into meeting his family again. This was fun.

Last week when she meet his mom again, it was like meeting an entirely different person. Scratch that. It was like meeting an entirely different family. Haley learned that his mom, Kate was a very warm and receptive woman, unlike Judith, who just wanted her son to be happy. She apologized countless times about the night she'd invited Callie to dinner. She immediately fell in love with Megan and showered her with gifts and referred to Megan as her granddaughter.

Brad wasn't kidding when he said that Megan would be spoiled.

Brad's brother's Brandon, and Bryan along with Bryan's wife and kids made Haley and Megan feel like part of the family. This is something that she always wanted, but never had. It was she always gave to Megan though, her unconditional love. She never wanted Megan to not feel loved, or was never good enough.

"What pictures?" Brandon, Brad's older brother inquired as he rounded the doorway leading into the hilarious show and tell. His smiling blue eyes looking at his mother then to Haley and finally resting on the photo album as his eyes widen momentarily, and feigned mock horror. Brandon looked just like Brad, dark hair, tall, muscular, expect for the eyes. Brandon must have gotten the same blue eyes from their mother. Brandon turned to Brad and placed his hand over his chest, like he sympathized with Brad's pain.

"Mom and dad having sex." Brad bluntly informed his brother. Brandon shot a glance to the photo album sprawled open on their mother's lap in mock disgust. "Ewe! Gross! You took pictures?"

"Bradley?" Kate scolded without taking her eyes from the albums situated before her.

"What?" He drew out trying to feign innocence while he desperately tried to hide his grin that was betraying him.

"Don't fill your brother's head with any ideas." She warned without looking away from the photos she was sharing with Haley.

"After all these years you still have a cute little behind," Haley whispered into his back as she wrapped her arms around him from behind, resting her cheek against his muscled back, smiling, a few hours later.

Brad let out an exasperated sigh. "She didn't really show those pictures? Did she?," he grumbled as he looked over his shoulder, towards her. From the way Haley's stomach was trembling against his back made it obvious that she did. He wondered if she knew the story his mother told her about that particular picture.

There was only one way to find out.

"Will you show me the full moon when we go home?" She whispered innocently.

Brad took that moment to turn himself in her arms. Her breath caught in her chest as he looked down at her with hooded seductive eyes. "I'll show you more than just the moon." His sexy implication sent waves of excitement through her. She rose up on her tippy toes, impelled involuntarily by her own passion as he hunched down wrapping his arms around her, holding her close as her lips captured his. The kiss was like smoldering heat that joins metal.

"Enough of that, unless your planning on giving me a grandchild." Kate playful pushed at Brad's arm while mockingly scolding them.

"Hmmm?" He hummed through a smile making his lips vibrated against hers after his mom walked past them. "Should we start now?" He asked through a seductive whisper as he cocked one eyebrow, suggestively, then slowly let it relax.

"Later." She tried to filter the willingness from her voice. She would love to have more children. She didn't want Megan growing up as an only child, but was now really the best time to think about starting a family?

"You promise, you'll give me more babies?" Brad asked as he pulled his himself away just enough to look into her eye. She opened her mouth to voice her concern, when Kate interrupted. She was never so thankful interruption.

"Oh! I almost to forgot to tell you." Kate started as she began to cover the leftovers. "Your cousin, Melanie is moving back home. Apparently she lost her job and her no good boyfriend got her into lots of trouble." Kate finished as she placed the last foil covered bowl into the refrigerator.

"What kind of trouble," Brad asked as he closed the refrigerator door before and handed Haley another bottle of iced tea.

"I'm not sure. You can ask her when you see her. She should be here on Friday. Daddy and I paid for her ticket to fly her home. Poor girl." Kate slowly shook her head in disgust.

"Is she going to be staying with her mom?" Brad asked after he lifted his own bottle of tea to his mouth and took a drink. She wished she had cousins. She probably did, but just didn't know where any of them were.

"Cathy's still upset with her and for good reason. So I told her she was more than welcomed to stay here with us until she can get on her feet again." Brad smiled fondly of his mom's generosity.

Brenda, Brad's sister pulled her and Brad away from Kate and the rest of the family and moved them into the living room, shortly after dinner.

Brenda sat down on the floral wingback chair, opposite the sofa matching the chair, where Brad and Haley sat.

A dejected expression shadowed over Brenda's face as she finally looked up from her clasped hands. The look on Brenda's face made Haley's stomach sink in despair as she shriveled a little at her expression.

This couldn't be good.

"Adam's attorney contacted me today." Brenda solemnly started out as crossed her legs, leaning into the side of the chair. She let out a heavy, troubled sigh before she continued. "Adam is seeking full custody of Megan."

Haley's expression was one of mute wretchedness as tears pooled in her eyes, choking her voice. A shock of defeat held her immobile. *He was taking her baby?*

"But I thought there was an order against him?" A dubious tone rose in Brad's voice.

Brenda raised her hands, gesturing for Brad to calm down while she continued. "There still is . . ."

"But!" He interrupted her vehemently.

"Brad you need to calm down. You're not helping." Brenda warned.

Brad quickly got to his feet, looking down at his sister and pointed an accusing finger at her. "How in the fuck do expect me to calm down when that asshole is threatening to take away my daughter? Huh? I love that little girl like she was my own." He lashed out in reckless anger.

Haley finally managed to find her voice. "Brad. Your sister's right. You need to calm down." She replied in a low, tormented voice.

Brad turned his attention to Haley and looked down at her. She could feel his penetrating stare boring into her. Swallowing the sob that rose in her throat, she looked up and gasped. His mocha eyes darkened like angry thunderclouds.

"Are you fucking serious?" Rancor hardened his voice.

"Calm down and listen to what your sister has to say." Her green eyes clawed at him like talons. She reacted angrily to the challenge in his voice. She knew Brad was upset, but he if he was going to help her, he needed to control his rage.

"Are you serious? He repeated with contempt. His face was a glowering mask of rage.

She gave him a hostile glare as she opened her mouth, but he cut her off. "I'll fucking relax, when that son of a bitch is dead!" His anger became scalding fury as he stomped towards the door, jerking it open, then slamming it shut.

The force of his seething reply took her off guard. She sat on the sofa, frozen with fear as she watched Brenda frantically run after her hot-headed brother.

*Oh! God!* Was Brad going to kill Adam?

# Chapter 19

"I don't care what you have to do to get it done. Just. Do It!" Adam bit out harshly as he gripped the SoHo glass between his thumb and middle finger. Swirling the amber shaded liquid until it sloshed around the sides of the crystal glass, before whipping his head back and draining the contains. He slammed the glass on the counter of the bar and enjoyed the slow burn of the whiskey before looking over at his brother. "Make it happen." He warned as he placed his foot on the rung of the barstool, getting ready to move.

"Do you know how much trouble I can get into falsifying police reports?" Danny's whispered as he slowly craned his neck and looked around the dimly lit lounge bar.

Adam looked over his brother's cautious features and scoffed to himself. And he called himself a police officer?

Puh-lease! He knew without a doubt anyone of the police officers could be corrupt, for the right price that is. To serve and to protect? He'd make sure Danny served him alright. He'd tarnish Haley's pristine past. Then he'd protect him, by taking the heat for falsifying police records. He didn't want to sue Haley for custody, but she didn't give he much of a choice. Now did she? *He* needed Megan. Not her. He was the one running for Governor and had a image to uphold. Not her. She could very easily make more babies with her brawny, dickhead of a husband.

Adam slipped his hand inside the breast pocket of his casual black linen jacket and slide a bulky, white envelope over to Danny.

Danny's finger's shook as he opened the flap and gasped. "Jesus! Christ! Adam!" He whispered in shock. "You can't buy me off."

"Anything can be bought, Danny." He informed gruffly as he adjusted his jacket and walked towards the exit.

Brad twisted the cap from the bottle of MGD and chucked it across the room as he leaned into the counter. The rattling of the little piece of metal on the shiny floor let him know he'd missed the trash can.

His clomping bare feet slapped against the cool, tiled floor and came to rest beside the trash can that situated beneath the window in the kitchen, framing the back yard. He tipped the bottle back, and took a long pull as his gazed aimlessly into the desolate yard.

Brad stood at Haley's kitchen window, with his thick, strong hands bracing himself against the frame. Since they were married, it just seemed easier and cheaper for him to move in with her.

She was hesitant at first because of Megan. He understood and was willing to wait as long as it took. It didn't mean that he liked it though. They had only been married for two weeks when he made the suggestion. But he didn't want to make her feel rushed or do anything to make Megan feel uncomfortable. They'd already suffered enough from the hands of Adam. They wouldn't suffer by him.

God! He loved the sound of that girls giggle. He could come home from work in a bad mood from the shitty day he had, but once Megan ran across the room and lunged into his arms, shrieking all the way, he could feel his mood shifting, quickly. He knew without a doubt that he would do whatever it took to protect his little girl.

He knew Megan wasn't biological his, but that didn't matter. She was daddy's little girl. He felt sorry for the son of bitch that tried to tell him any different.

"Brad." The sound of his name rolling from her mouth made him smile. He was more relaxed than he was earlier when he stormed out of his mother's house. He was pissed at everything and everybody. More so he was pissed at Adam. Because of him, Haley had to live in constant fear of Adam taking away the one thing that meant the most to her.

He wanted to so bad hunt Adam down and beat the shit out of him before he strangled him. He'd take great pride into watching the life drain out of him. The same way he drained the life out of Haley.

"There you are!" Shrieked Megan as she ran to him. Her chestnut hair flowing all around her.

"Did you miss me, Munchkin?" Brad asked as he placed a kiss on her cheek after he scooped her up in his arms.

"Yes!" She informed him brightly with a wide smile on her face. "But you made mommy sad." She whispered as her tiny finger toyed with the hoop earring in his ear.

He felt a stab of guilt in the pit of his stomach. "How did I make mommy sad?" He shifted her in his arms, that way her little legs were draped along his side with his arms wrapped around her back as he watched her. "Mommy cried on Aunt Brenda's shoulder after you left." Megan told him in a pouty tone, further making him feel like an ass.

"Do you think we should cheer mommy up?" Megan whipped her head up, glee twinkling in her green eyes as her mouth popped open, revealing an excited smile as she nodded in agreeance.

"Haley? Honey? Megan and I will be back in a little bit." He called out as he headed towards the back door. He didn't give her time to protest it.

Before she could respond, Brad was out the door with Megan. He probably didn't want to hear her lecture again. It would've probably went in one ear and out the other anyways. So he saved her the time and energy. And right now she could use all the energy she could get. She was so tired all of the time. But wouldn't be with all the drama that was going on in her life.

She decided to run herself a nice hot bath since Brad had Megan. She could relax and unwind. She knew without a doubt that Brad wouldn't let anything happen to her. He was even more protective of Megan than she was. But that was a good thing. Megan needed someone like Brad in her life. Someone that was going to care for her, not care what she could do for him. Unlike Adam who only cared that Megan smiled big for the camera.

After her bath she decided to dress in the most comfortable pair of pajama's that she owned. A camisole top and flannel pants. So what if they weren't sexy. When she was around Brad, it didn't matter what she was wearing, he still found her desirable. That was taking her some time to get used to.

"Mommy!" Megan shrieked as she ran towards her holding a bouquet of roses. "Who are these for?" Haley asked after she placed her bookmark in the book she was currently reading and turned her attention to her daughter. "There for you, Mommy." The excitement danced in Megan's green eyes as Haley took the flowers from her and then placed them on the vacant cushion next to her. Haley turned her attention back to Megan and opened her arms. Megan didn't hesitate as she climbed up on Haley's lap and wrapped her arms around her neck.

Haley closed her eyes and gently rocked Megan back and forth as her hands glided along Megan's small back.

God! She hoped Brenda's plan worked by asking the judge for a motion to delay the custody hearing. Brenda also made the suggestion of hiring a Private Investigator to look into Adam's past. Haley readily agreed to anything that would help them out. There was no way she'd ever be able to life without Megan in her life. She willed herself not to cry as she embraced Megan tighter.

The sound of rustling plastic drew her attention. She opened her eyes and blinked away the tears that threatened and looked over her shoulder to the source of the noise.

Brad picked the bouquet up and motioned towards the kitchen. She nodded her head and mouthed the words thank-you to him. He gave her an impish grin that was just for her and nodded his head before walking through the doorway. Megan and her were so lucky to have him in their life's. She just hoped that things would forever remain that way.

# Chapter 20

"Is she asleep?" Haley asked as Brad approached the end of their bed, making his way over to his side.

"Yes. I don't know who was more tired. Megan or my mom?" Kate took Megan amusement park for the day. Megan beamed with excitement when Brad and Haley went to pick her up from his mom's house. Her little arms hugged the assortment of stuffed animals to her chest.

Brad informed her with a smirk after he dropped his shirt to the floor. Haley felt her mouth slack. Could one really lust after their own husband like this?

Yes they could.

Brad caught her gaze boldly raking over him as she stared at him shamelessly. Her eyes slowly and seductively trailed across his tanned, mammothed chest, along his defined six pack abs and ended at the prominent V temptingly poking out from his jeans that rested low on his hips. She noticeable swallowed when she discovered the button to his jeans were undone.

She couldn't help but smile as she looked over his dragon tattoo and felt herself flush as the memories of the other night when she ran her tongue across it. She would never forget the heated look in his eyes or the incredible loving making they'd done shortly afterwards.

"Do you like what you see? Mrs. Tyson?" His deep voice dropped down an octave. Not Barry White low, but just enough to convey sexy. Her eyes slowly followed the same gorgeous path they'd just taken moments ago and looked into smoldering flames that startled her. Her heart jotted and her pulse pounded as she licked her suddenly dry lips. His flames stoked the fire that was burning within her.

"Yes." She replied breathlessly as she watched him slowly unzip his pants. Liquid heat pooled between her legs when he tossed his boxer briefs to the floor and stood by her side of the bed in all his glory.

"There seems to be a problem here." He gave her his irresistible sexy grin of his that made her ache with need.

"What's that?" She moaned as she closed her eyes and laud her head to the side as leaned over her, supporting his weight on his forearms as he placed open mouth kisses on her neck.

"You have too many clothes on." He mumbled against her sensitized skin before he pulled his mouth away from her and slowly stood up, hooking his thumbs into her pajama pants and pulled them down her legs along with her panties and tossed them over his shoulder.

He hunched down enough to shift her on the bed so that way her legs draped over the edge and then stood back up as he teasingly ran his finger tips along the inside of her thigh, down her calves and ending at her ankles, making her shiver.

His strong, thick hands gently massaged her feet as he placed open mouth kisses against her ankle. He continued his ministration until he reached her juncture.

His warmth breath feathered across her mound as his finger traced her slit.

"Brad please." She moaned as she swirled her hips.

"Please what?" He whispered as he kissed her mound.

"I want you." She didn't even recognize her own voice, she was so needy.

"You have me." He informed her as he settled between her legs tossing them over his shoulders.

"I want you inside me. Now!" She breathlessly demanded as she rolled her hips again.

"Not until I get what I want." His warm breath feathered against her wet fold as he spread her lips and flicked his tongue against her swollen nub.

"What do you want?" She moaned as she arched her back. "I want to hear you scream my name." Before she could even try to respond to his request she felt herself tighten as he pushed a finger inside in. He tongue was relentless and his finger was demanded as she felt herself spiraling out of control. Another flick of his tongue, her control scatter as clawed at the sheets underneath her and screamed his name as her orgasm ripped through her.

"I love watching you come undone." Brad's husky voice prolonged the spasms rippling through her as he trusted into her, causing her to cry out. He silenced her cries as he captured her mouth and continued to trusted into her. She wrapped her hands around his back and held him close. His unyielding, hard trust caused her nails bit into back as she could feel another orgasm building.

His thrusting stopped long enough for him to sit back on his hunches, never breaking their precious contact as he tilted her hip then quickly picked up his pace. She hooked her legs around his back.

"Come for me, baby." He whispered harshly making her back arch of the bed as she scream his name for t he second time, her nails digging into his outer thighs as continued to pound into her. Heavy panting feathered against her neck when he pressed his head against hers and buried his face into her hair and growled deep from his chest. She felt his muscles tightened as he gave three quick thrust, releasing his seed.

Brad settled on top of her, resting his weight on his forearms that cradled her head. He placed gentle and tender kisses on her lips. As gentle a warm summer breeze. Raising his mouth from hers, he gazed into her eyes. "I love you." He whispered. Haley ran her hands through his hair and smiled. "I love you, too." She whispered back. His lips recaptured her, more demanding this time as he swirled his hips making her gasp.

"Again?"

"Oh, yeah baby." He smiled as he whispered against her neck, as he slowly began trusting into her. She was going to be so sore tomorrow, but it would be more than worth it.

"Hello?"

"Haley. It's Brenda."

"Oh hey. What's up? I didn't recognize your number." Haley cradled the phone against her moist cheek as she readjusted her towel.

"That's because I'm calling you from my office." Brenda explained. "Listen, I wanted to let you know now the judge had granted the motion and our guy found some pretty interesting stuff on Adam."

Haley's hand clutched her chest, silently gesturing her relief. "That's such a relief. What sort of stuff did he find out."

"I don't know yet. I'm meeting with him in a couple of hours. I'll keep you posted.

"Thank-you so much for everything Brenda. I don't think I would've been able to get through this without your help."

"Hey, that's what sister's are for. Love ya. Talk to ya soon." Haley disconnected the call as strong arms wrapped around her from behind, making her smile. "What about my help?" Brad asked in a rather sexy, but pouty voice as he nibbled on her earlobe making her giggle.

She turned to face him and wrapped her arms around his neck, standing on her tippy-toes, she sought out his lips. "You've been very helpful." She said between kisses.

"Glad to hear it. What did Brenda have to say?" He asked as his hands held onto her back. Haley went over the conversation with him, not letting any detail out.

"Well, hopefully this guy can shed some light into Adam's past that will help our case.

"I hope so too."

Brad pulled away from her, just enough to look in her eyes. His expression was unreadable. She could feel herself tense up. "What's wrong?" She asked, concern evident in her voice, her eyes narrowing suspiciously.

"I was just wondering after this Adam thing is over, If I can adopt Megan?" He said the words tentatively as if testing the idea. His eyes clung to hers, analyzing her reaction. She felt a warm glow flow through her as her smile broadened in approval.

"Really?" He pressed her with relentless enjoyment. Tenderly, his mocha eyes melted in hers.

Before she could respond, he reclaimed her lips, crushing her to him. She returned the kiss with reckless abandon. "Yes, really." She said breathlessly a few moments later, as her chest heaved.

A mischievous look came into his eyes. The smile that matched the spark in his eyes was boyishly affectionate

"What?"The beginning of a smile tipped the corners of her mouth as she tossed her head to the side and eyed him mock suspicion.

"I'm going to go tell her the good news!" Wild enthusiasm flourished through his eager tone as he bound from their bedroom and headed straight from Megan in living room.

Her heart sang with delight as she found herself grinning from ear to ear. Her euphoria was quickly scattered and was replaced with a sourness in the pit of her stomach. Would Adam ever allow Megan to carry her husband's last name? Nausea tore through her as she slapped her hand across her mouth and ran towards the bathroom.

She really despised Adam Lucas.

# Chapter 21

"Great news!" Brenda exclaimed as shoved through the door, just as Brad begun to open it. Her hurried past him, not stopping to explain why she just barged in.

"Please. Come in." Brad's tongue was heavy with sarcasm as he watched his sister's retreating back move further into the living room. He closed the door and strolled over to the couch and resumed his seat with Megan. He looked down at her and watched in amazement as she stared at the television screen, unfazed by her Aunt's sudden appearance.

Brad glanced to the television and inwardly scoffed. No wonder why she hadn't moved. Whenever Barbie was on, she tuned anything and everything out. Just the other day he had to turn the program off just to get her to come into the kitchen to eat supper. She looked up at him, bottom lip quivering, while giving him the innocent doe-looking expression.

He was such a sucker for that lip, and she knew. As soon as he promised to play dress-up with her, her face lit up brighter than the rising sun, vigorously nodding her head in approval. Just like he made her promise not to tell anyone about the about the hot pink boa, and the cherry red lipstick he wore. Especially not mommy.

A man had to maintain is pride.

"I'm going to go visit with Auntie B." He informed her as he placed a kiss on top of her head. When she didn't respond to him, he wasn't surprised.

"How are two of my favorite ladies doing?" He asked as he walked past the kitchen table, towards the cupboard and reached inside for a glass.

"Brad what are you doing to her? She looks like crap." Brenda asked accusingly.

Brad looked over his shoulder as he poured himself a glass of iced tea. "I'm not doing anything to her." He said defensively. And he wasn't doing anything to her . . . yet.

He looked from his sister than to Haley. Her normal tanned completion was slightly paled, and she had traces of black circles under her eyes.

Was she sick? He vaguely remember her saying something about her stomach this morning.

"Babe? Are you sick?" Concern was in his voice as he placed a hand against her forehead. He didn't even wait for her to respond as he glared over his shoulder towards his sister. "What did *you* do to her?" he bit out sharply.

"Me!?" Brenda demanded as she placed a hand against her chest, gesturing her shock. "She looks the way I felt when I found out I was pregnant with Connor."

Pregnant? He whirled his attention back to Haley and looked down at her. The numbness of his sister's words choose that time to sink in. That hadn't used any form of birth control since they married.

Haley quickly pushed his hand away. "I'm not pregnant Brad. I just ate something that didn't agree with me."

"Okay." He said cautiously as he slowly backed away from her and grabbed his glass from the counter before pulling out a chair and joined his sister and wife at the table. He kept looking over at her. Every time she catch his eye, she quickly advert her eyes to her hands and twisted her hands around in her lap.

He might be new to this whole marriage thing, but he wasn't an idiot. She was keeping something from him. And he was going to find out.

She could have kicked Brenda in shin under the table for mentioning the whole pregnancy thing. She was starting to mentally agree with her and was going to say just that, until she seen that look in Brad's eyes. Seeing the raw panic glittering in his dark eyes, aroused old fears and insecurities with that look.

Besides, it was hard to say whether she might be pregnant or not. She couldn't remember the last time she had a period, but with all the stress she was under, was it any wonder? Maybe Brenda could help alleviate some of the tension.

"So what did you find out?" She sounded hopeful. She was eager to learn what the private investigator found out about Adam, but also desperately needed to change the subject.

Brenda let out a heavy sigh. "Well." She started out as she reached down into her briefcase and plopped down a thick manila folder on the table before opening it up. "Do you know a man by the name of Jeff Clark?" Brenda asked as her eyes continued to look over the papers in her hands.

"No." She answered honestly. It didn't sound familiar at all.

"He used to date your former babysitter? What was her name?" Brenda voices trailed off as she searched for the paper that had the former sitters name on it.

"Janice Welliver." Haley answered bitterly.

"Yes. That would be her name."

"Okay? What does the private investigator's investigation have to do with Janice?" Haley asked, not understanding where Brenda was going with this.

Brenda tossed the papers back onto the file and leaned back into the kitchen chair as she regarded Haley. There was a pensive shimmer in the shadows of her eyes.

"Brenda?" Concern etched in her voice. "What aren't you telling me." She felt her composure was under attack.

"Okay. I'm going to be frank here." Brenda said after she cleared her throat.

"Good! Please do." Brad informed his sister smugly.

Brenda narrowed her gaze at Brad. "What I'm about to tell you, you have to remain calm." Brenda stressed to Brad.

"Cut the shit, Brenda. And just get to it." Brad bit out, impatiently.

Brenda cocked her head to the side and gave him a warning glare. "Brad. Please." Haley pleaded as she reached across the table and laced her fingers with his. He looked over at her and then raised his their joined hands as he placed a kiss on the top of her hand. "Anything for you, babe."

They both turned their attention to Brenda and stared at her expectantly. "Jeff Clark works for Adam Lucas. When Adam realized he was going to be getting a lot of attention of the media and his opponent would with a doubt dig into his past, he knew he'd have to correct his prior decisions. He couldn't just pop up in your life's after all these years. So, he decided to take matters into his own hands."

Brad shifted around in his chair but didn't say anything as Haley looked to him and then back to Brenda. "What do you mean took matters into his own hands?" Uncertainty made her voice hard and demanding.

"Jeff was sent to your house the night Megan was hurt." As soon as Brenda mentioned that night, Haley felt her stomach tighten as an odd primitive warning sounded in her mind. Her heart started drumming in her ears. "When Adam found out you were at work, he sent Jeff over there in hopes of Janice letting me in the door. When he gained his entry, he drugged Janice and staged the area to make it look like Janice had gotten herself drunk."

"Why would he do that?"

Brenda was silent for a few moments as she closed her eyes, as if she was pained to continue. "Brenda?" Haley prompted. She took a deep breath before continuing. "Adam wanted something bad to happen to Megan that way he'd have leverage on you."

"Why not just kidnap her?" Haley shouted in outrage as tears streamed down her cheeks. Brad rose for the table and moved to stand behind her chair. He softly placed his hands on her shoulders. Hushed curses fell from his mouth.

"He needed something to hang over your head to convince to you marry him." A sudden chill hung on the edge of her words. Adam planned the whole vile incident to occur? He was the reason her little girl almost died that night. Fury almost choked her as she only half listened as she struggled with realization that Adam planned this horrific attack against her. He just proved that he would stop at nothing to achieve what *he* wanted. Even if that meant sacrificing his own flesh and blood.

She was suddenly anxious to escape from this disturbing conversation. Her stomach was on board with the idea as well, when she felt her it roll and churn.

"I'm gonna be sick!" Haley shoved her chair back and ran to the bathroom as the scolding hot tears slipped down her cheeks.

Brad saw red as his fingers tightened around the back of the wooden chair. The fury Brad was feeling right then was like nothing he'd ever felt before. He somehow managed to stand true to Haley, when he promised to remain calm. But that didn't mean that he didn't want to beat the shit out of the spineless bastard that put his own flesh and body in jeopardy. *His*, little girl, and then was going to point the blame at Haley if she didn't agree to marry him?

He jaw clenched as he plopped back down into his chair, his leg bounced under the table, making the cream table cloth shift around his jerky movements. He knew he should be checking on Haley, or holding his little girl, but he needed to know more.

He took a deep breath and willed himself to relax as best as he could. "How did your guy find all this out?" As he asked he slouched back in his chair and folded his arms across his chest.

Brenda finished taking a sip of her coffee, and replaced it to the table before she responded. "Jeff Clark told everything to my guy. When I contacted him and asked him if he'd go to the police and give a statement, he flat out refused."

"Why?"

"I wondered the same thing and had a friend of mine at the police station do an background check on him." Brenda's paused as she looked down at the table.

"And!"

"It seems, Jeff is Adam's go to guy. Since Adam doesn't want to get his hands dirty he has Jeff do it for a price."

"If the police know this, why haven't they arrested him."

"There's that little thing called evidence and since Adam's brother works at the police station. You do the math there genius."

"Son of a bitch." He bit out harshly.

"Okay? Then why did he tell your guy everything we needed to know?"

"It appears Adam and Jeff had a falling out. Jeff wasn't afraid to tell my guy everything. It would be his word against John's if there was ever any heat from Adam. He could easily deny saying anything.

"Shit. If only John had recorded the conversation."

A mischievous eyebrow rose up her forehead as a impish grin tipped the corner of her mouth. "Who says he didn't?"

# Chapter 22

Haley tried for calms breaths, even though she was anything but calm. Her legs felt wobbly, as if they were ready to give out any minute now as she slowly climbed the steps leading into the courthouse. This was it. This was the day the Judge would hopefully make his ruling for custody of Megan. She should feel ecstatic, like she was walking on air. She felt confident enough knowing that if this judge had a lick of common sense he wouldn't grant Adam custody. But instead she felt like her legs were like a bowl full of Jell-O and her stomach fluttered with butterflies.

"You two will wait right here." Brenda informed Haley and Brad as she swung a door wide open, gesturing for them to step inside. Haley cautiously walked in as her eyes scanned the small area while her fingers curled tightly around her purse strap that rested on her shoulder.

"How long will this take?" Haley asked distractedly, as she pulled out a padded chair.

"It depends. If Adam's lawyer agrees to the terms, than not long. I have a feeling he's going to try and drawl this out. But with the evidence I have against his client, the chances of that happening are slim to none."

Haley drew in a deep breath. "I hope so." She said through a heavy sigh.

After Brenda left, Brad sat in the chair next to her and scooped her hand in his. His thumb lazily traced against her knuckles. "Everything will be alright, babe." Brad whispered in a reassuring tone. "Brenda knows what she doing."

It wasn't Brenda's reputation that worried her. It was Adam's immoral ways. Brenda had learned that Adam blackmailed his own brother into falsifying police records, to make it appear that she harmed Megan that horrible night. Danny took the heat and was reprimanded and threatened to be blacklisted if he never gave into his brother's selfish ways again.

Adam's self-centered ways knew no boundaries. When something, or someone got in his way, he'd persuade that something, or someone with money. She'd always heard money was the root of all evil, Adam just confirmed that theory. She just hoped the judge wasn't corrupt and could be easily persuaded.

"Did you really doubt me for one minute?" Brenda asked with a wicked glint in her eyes as she reached across their mother's table to spoon potato salad onto her plate, waiting for her to respond. As Haley watched Brenda slowly assemble her plate, her stomach begun to churn at the sight of food.

Kate decided to quickly throw together a celebration party after they arrived back at her house to get Megan. Kate was beyond thrilled when she learned Adam signed his rights away, making it easier for Brad to adopt Megan.

"No!" Haley shook her head, unconcerned. "I just wasn't too sure about Adam. I still can't believe he agreed to everything." Haley informed Brenda in a disbelieving tone. "Well, believe it or not. But Judge Martin didn't really give him any choice, but to agree."

With the admission of Jeff's taped confusion used as evidence, Judge Martin denied Adam custody and awarded

Haley with sole custody. Adam also had to agree to signing his rights away. He was never to be around Megan due to his hanis, selfish, behavior.

Brenda informed everybody that once this news hit the media, Adam would be forced to withdraw his campaign. Even if he didn't agree, he'd lose votes very fast. Nobody wanted a Governor that placed his own needs before others.

Brenda moved back to her seat and placed her plate in front of her, fork in hand, ready to dig in. A generous amount of potato salad clung to her fork, as she held it up, gesturing a toast "To Judge Martin." Brenda began and then pulled her fork from her mouth between pressed lips and chewed happily.

"To Judge Martin." Brad and Haley said in unison with raised forks, following trend of the toast. Haley's fork hovered at her lips as she begun to feel her mouth water, but it had nothing to do with being hungry from smelling the delicious food right before her nose.

Her mouth watered from a wave of nausea that rushed through her. She dropped her fork, causing it to make a clanging noise as it landed on her untouched plate.

"Excuse me." Haley voice was hurried as she jumped from her chair and made a mad dash to the bathroom. She strolled over to the mirror after she emptied the contains of her stomach and noted her unusually paleness. Dark circles shadowed under her eyes. It was probably from all the uncertainty from the day she had.

"Haley?" Uneasiness etched in his deep voice, followed by soft knocking on the door. He didn't even wait for her to open the door, before he pushed through, peeking around the door until his mocha eyes landed on her.

"Are you okay?" He asked as his dark eyebrows arched, gesturing his concern as he closed the door and walked towards her.

"Yeah. I think my nerves are still a bit frazzled from how things could've gone today." She said as she leaned into his hands that where cradling her face.

"Are you sure?" He whispered as he leaned into to place a kiss on her mouth. She felt his nearness and suddenly back away from him. "You don't want to kiss me. I just got sick." She warned him as she kept a hand pressed on his chest, keeping him away. He wrapped his hand around her wrist and moved it to his back as he closed the distance between them. "I took my vows seriously," he whispered as he placed a soft kiss on the tip of her nose. "In sickness." He began as he placed another soft kiss on her left cheek. She let her eyes flutter closed. "And in health." He continued as he kissed her other cheek. Feeling satisfied with himself, he placed a soft kiss on her parted lips. It was a kiss for her tired soul to melt into.

She broke the kiss as another wave of nausea rush through her. Expect for this time nausea brought a friend along. Light headedness.

Her palm flattened against her forehead as she slowly moved around in the small bathroom, until she sat on the closed lid of the toilet. Brad kept his hand on her until she was seated.

"Are you sure you're alright?" Brad asked as he looked up at her from his knelt position.

Haley slowly nodded head as she closed her eyes, willing the sensation to pass as quickly as it came. After a few silent moments, her eyes opened and she looked down in Brad's brown eyes that held hers with concern. She felt ready to try and stand. Everybody was probably wondering by now of what was keeping them. Brad stood as well, he looked down at her, a shadow of doubt flickered in his eyes, before he turned and opened the door for her. He extended his hand, gesturing for her to step out of the bathroom first. She slowly nodded her head again. As she neared the threshold, the same dizzying sensation rushed through her, causing her to stumble back against Brad's chest, before everything started to fade into darkness.

# Chapter 23

"I'm sure everything's fine." Brandon, Brad's older brother casual informed him as they sat Haley's room, breaking into the silence that surrounded them. She had to be okay. He told myself as he ran both his hands through his hair as he slowly strolled over to the window, looking down to the dimly lit parking lot of the hospital. He noted the parking lot held few less cars than it two hours ago when they first arrived.

Images of Haley's slumped lifeless body laying against him flashed into his mind. He panicked as he slowly lowered her to the floor, while he called out her name, as he lightly tapped her face with his fingers, willing her to snap out of whatever was wrong with her.

When she didn't respond to his voice or his touch, he freaked out and started yelling for someone to call for help.

By the time the paramedics arrived, Brandon had to pull Brad from her, so they could tend to her. He couldn't remember ever crying a day in his life, but he sure remembered crying like a baby as the paramedics lifted her lifeless body onto the stretcher.

Was she sick? He noticed that she wasn't eating a lot as of lately, but she reassured him that it was just her nerves from the impending custody battle against Adam when he confronted her about her eating habits changing.

He knew she had gotten sick a few times as well, but she reassured him again it was just her nerves. Something was wrong. He wasn't a doctor, but he just knew. He just hoped and prayed it was nothing too serious. They could finally take the next step into legally making Megan his daughter, and he was looking forward to making more babies with Haley. She just had—

"Brad?" Hearing Haley hoarsely whisper his name pulled him from his miserable thought as he turned to see she her struggling to sit up in her bed.

"Where am I?" She asked in a daze as she slowly looked around the room.

"You're in the hospital, baby" He informed her as he rushed to her side, helping her sit up while adjusting the pillow behind her.

"What am I doing here?" He noticed her cheeks were filling with their normal color as he looked her over as he sat down beside her on the bed, lacing his fingers with hers.

"Do you remember anything from back at mom's house?" She dropped her eyes to the sheet that covered her as she aimlessly looked around, trying to remember.

"I remember—" Haley was cut off as the door to her room swung open. Dr. Carter, the emergency room doctor looked over to Haley, as his eyes lit up.

"Good. You're awake." He beamed as he closed the door behind him and moved over the other side of the room, were a computer monitor was fastened to the wall. He gave the mouse a quick flick, creating a blue screen appear.

"How are you feeling?" Dr. Carter asked as he being tapping against the keyboard, removing the blue screen and replacing it with a white one.

"Alright. I guess." Haley informed him as she shifted around in her bed.

"Good. Good." Dr. Carter didn't look away from the computer as he continued. Different images reflected off of Dr. Carter's glasses as he shifted from one screen to another.

"Doctor? Do you know what made my wife pass out?" Haley's hand tensed under his when he asked the question.

"Yes." This time when he responded, he turned his attention to the both of them as he leaned his back against the tan wall, and folded his arms across his white doctor's coat.

"It seems your wife was severely dehydrated from all the vomiting she'd done recently, but she's responding well from the treatment." Dr. Carter gestured towards Haley with a fond smile on his face.

"Do you know what caused her to be sick?" Brad asked sounding unsure. He wanted to know what was wrong with her, but he feared what he'd be learning.

"Yes. She's suffering from hyperemesis grauidarum."

Brad sent him a perplexed look. "Ah? Doc? Laymen's terms please?"

"I'm sorry." Dr. Carter said through a rueful smile. "Please forgive me." He placed a hand on his chest, gesturing his apology. "Your wife is suffering from a serve case of morning sickness?"

Morning sickness? Didn't woman have that when they were—

Pregnant? Haley was pregnant?

He whipped his head in her direction. Instead of looking into her beautiful green eyes, he was looking at the top of her head. Shiny strands of her chestnut hair lay against her slumped shoulders as she continued to look down at her lap. He noticed her hands twisted the edge of the blanket that covered her.

He hesitated. He wanted to pull her into his arms and kiss her all over, and thank her for making this day even better. But he needed to know more.

"Can you give her something to make the sickness go away?"

"I've already prescribe a medicine that will ease her sickness, but it won't make the sickness go away. It will just be easier for her to hold down food and liquids"

Brad absently nodded his head, as more questions circulated around in his head. Dr. Carter gladly answered all of Brad's inquires and answered some he hadn't even though of.

"I'd like to do an ultra sound, just to how far along she is."

Brad nodded his head as he focused his attention to Haley, how was now aimlessly looking around the room, but avoiding him.

What the hell? Was she upset that she was pregnant again? She always changed the subject when he mentioned about having more babies with her.

She didn't want the baby?

"Do you need anything else before I leave?" Brad softy asked her as he placed a glass of ginger ale on the coffee table and ran his hand over her forehead, brushing away the strands that had collected.

"No. I'm good thank-you." She started to lean up on her elbow to kiss him, when he stopped her.

"I'll come to you." That sexy grin formed on his face as she lowered herself back down onto the cushion. Brad braced his arms on the couch, as he lowered his head, and captured her lips. His kiss was surprising gentle.

"I'll see you later. Call me if you need anything." He said as he righted himself, while still facing her. He placed his hand on her stomach, ever so gently and begun to rub.

It's something that he did every morning before he left for work, and every night before they went to sleep. It didn't matter where she was, he'd find her. She could be in the shower and he'd reach in to rub "his" baby. The first week after they learned she was pregnant, she found his affection for their unborn child sweet and very heart warming. Three weeks later, she was finding it a tad annoying.

During the ultrasound, they learned that Haley was nine weeks along in her pregnancy. They both guessed the first night they meet, is about the time she got pregnant. Guessed what happened in Vegas, didn't always stay in Vegas.

But, she wouldn't change it for the world. The day she was discharged from the hospital, she was scared senseless. She was scared because she was pregnant. She was overjoyed to be having another baby, but she was terrified Brad would leave her. She knew he wasn't Adam. Far from it. But, deep down inside she was preparing herself for him to abandon her. It's all she knew.

Her mother wanted nothing to do with her when she was pregnant with Megan, as did Adam. Sure in the beginning he was excited, but his mother, Judith planted the seed of doubt in his mind. Telling Adam that the baby wasn't his.

Judith won that battle. Which was for the best, after all. When they finally arrived home, she broke down and voice her concerns with Brad. He promised her he'd never leave her, or their children behind. He enforced his endearments by telling her, Megan and her were stuck with him.

Such torture?

"Daddy loves you." He whispered to her belly before placing a soft kiss just right below her belly button. He gave her a chaste kiss before going in the kitchen in search of "his" little girl, giving her kiss before leaving.

She felt beyond blessed and extremely happy that her dreams where finally coming true. If she was so happy, then why couldn't she shake the feeling of impending doom?

# Chapter 24

A faint background noise hummed in her ears waking her up. She blinked her eyes open, rubbing away the sleep. She must have dozed off, she sleepily thought as her eyes adjusted to the flickers of light bounced off the tan carpet in her living room as the television show jumped from scene-to-scene, in the dark room.

She didn't remember turning on the television, she idly thought as she rolled to her side and stared at the screen. She let out a bored sigh as light from the television continued to shimmer as the programming switched to a commercial about batteries.

Haley silenced a yawn with the back of her hand as she watched a pink bunny whirl around on the screen. Tonight

Brad had Megan with him. He'd played poker with his brother's ever Wednesday. They'd switch places ever week, one week would be at their house, and the next Brandon's and then Bryan's.

Megan begged him, as she stuck out her lower lip, making it tremble, for good measure, to go to Brandon's house with him, since she absolutely loved to play with her cousins. When that didn't work for her, she decided to change tactics that would guarantee an evening with her Daddy.

Tears.

Brad, being the sucker that he was, caved as soon as the first tears slipped down her cheek.

Just as her eyes gently shut they immediately sprang open as a ghastly smash had her curling up her legs, and tucking her head down as her arms wrapped protectively around her head as a torrent burst of debris rained down on her. She felt something odd land on her hip before tense silence enveloped the room. She remained motionless for what seemed hours as she listened closely. The only sounds she heard was her heart frantically drumming in her ears and her heavy panting against the hunter green throw blanket that she somehow managed to pull over her head.

When she didn't hear anything she slowly pulled the cover down, exposing just her eyes to peek around the room.

What the hell? Why was there light beaming at her? Shimmering from the television reflected on shards of glass that littered her living room carpet. She slowly crept up onto the couch supported herself on her elbow as she craned her neck to look up behind her and frowned. The middle section of her three paned window was gone and now scattered across her floor. Splinter marks looking like tiny see-through veins etched in the remaining windows. She let out a sigh as she turned her attention back to the floor as she slowly began to remove the blanket, beginning careful of the tiny shards of glass that may have collected on the cover. Something shifting around on her hip had her looking to her side. A large piece of glass with razor-sharp edges was resting on her. She swallowed loudly as her eyes began to fill with tears, thinking what might of happened had she not rolled to her side beforehand.

Is that what maternal instincts were about? A warning of something bad happening before it happened?

She refused to cry about something that did not happen. She was just very grateful and thanking her guardian angel watched from above, allowing nothing happened to her or her unborn child. She protectively patted her stomach before she finished sitting up.

Carefully pushing the blanket to the opposite end of the couch, she searched the inside of her shoes before slipping her feet inside. After she tied her shoes she gradually rose from the couch and moved towards the center of the room. Her gaze moved back and forth from the mess scattered across her floor to the damaged window.

How in the hell did this happen? It was a nice day outside so maybe the neighbor mowed from across the street, and caused a rock to hurtle her way. No. Today was Wednesday. Cliff, her neighbor only mowed on Thursday's. If happened to rain the day he mowed, he simply waited until the following Thursday. She never asked why he only mowed on Thursday's. As different scenarios drifted through her mind, something caught her attention in the middle of the mess.

Was that a . . . brick? Her eyebrows furrowed as she neared the square, rust colored block. She stood mere inches away from the slab as her eyes searched the window and then back to the brick. As she was moving her eyes away from the brick to look at the window, again something odd caught her attention.

Why would there be a rubber band wrapped around a brick? She slowly looked around the room and then to the window before she carefully knelt down to pick it up. She turned the brick over and found a white piece of paper tucked between the brick and rubber band.

Should she remove the paper? Her stomach twisted into a knot as her trembling fingers untangled the thick blue band. A wave of apprehension swept over her as the rustling of paper cut into the heavy silence surrounded her. She closed her eyes and let out a breath she didn't realize she was holding. The paper that was clutched tightly in her fingers moments ago, slowly floated to the floor as Haley slapped her hands over her mouth, trying to silence her frightened gasp as tears began to collect in her eyes.

The bold black alarming letters stared up at her, revealing the chilling threat . . . **YOU'RE GOING TO REGRET THIS!!**

# Chapter 25

Haley sat on a cushioned wooden chair in her kitchen as Officer Stanley leaned his back against the counter jotting down her statement into the little black notepad he held in his hands.

Her fingers pulled at the tiny white piece of thread that rested against the uneven texture of the placemat situated before her on the round walnut dinette table as Brad shifted around in his chair, uncomfortably as he crossed his arms over his chest as he aimlessly looked around the kitchen.

"Where do you work, Mrs. Tyson?"

"At the hospital."

"Doing what?"

"I work in labor and delivery as a registered nurse. Why?" He asked her if there was anybody that she works with that might hold a grudge. When Haley couldn't think of anybody, she nodded her head.

"Where were you at Mr. Tyson when this incident occurred?" Brad jerked his attention to Officer Stanley, his expression dazed "What?!" He retorted, outraged.

"Where were you when—?"

"Yeah! I got that part!" He replied in reckless anger. "I was with my brother's playing cards." He replied in a low voice, taut with anger.

"Where does your brother live?" Officer Stanley inquired as he continued to write in his notepad, not bothering to address Brad as he spoke. His accusing tone sliced into the tensed air.

"Are you accusing me of something?" He glared at Officer Stanley with burning, reproachful eyes, as his arm swung out, gesturing towards the living where the broken glass still remained.

"Mr. Tyson," Officer Stanley started out in an appeasing tone. "No one is accusing you of anything."

"Yeah, well. It certainly doesn't seem like. Now does it?" Brad demanded as he got to his feet and walked towards the refrigerator.

"Is there anyone else you can think of that might have a grudge against you?" The question was directed at Haley.

"Yeah! Adam fucking Lucas." Brad snapped, cutting Haley off.

"The same Adam Lucas that was running for Governor? Officer Stanley asked, not sounded surprised.

"One in the same."

"Why would Adam Lucas have a grudge against you or your family?" Officer Stanley sounded amused as he continued to write in his notebook.

Both Haley and Brad explained the whole Adam situation to the Officer and an hour later, when the rest of the police officers had all the information and evidence they needed, they were going to give dear ole' Adam visit.

"Maybe I'm going to have to hire a body guard for you make Megan when I'm not home." Brad suggested after he came into their bedroom, after tucking Megan into bed for the night.

"We don't need security." Haley said sounding unconcerned. Yes, she was scared shitless tonight that someone had vandalized their house, but not scared enough to have someone watching over her every move.

"That's what I have you for." Haley whispered as she glided her hands against Brad's bare back. She immediately felt his back tense under her touch.

"Haley. I'm serious." He warned "I need to know that you, Megan and this little one are safe when I'm not around." He turned to face her as he dropped his hand down to her stomach. Once he began to rub her belly, she could feel him starting to relax.

She cupped her hands around his face and lifted his head until his eyes where level with hers. "Everything's going to be okay. Officer Stanley said they'd patrol this area more. We'll be alright." She lifted her face until her lips meet his.

She broke their kiss a few moments later. Feeling out of breath she looked into his dark brown eyes that softened at the sight of her.

"You know. When I first meet you that night Keith drunk knocked on your door, I couldn't get you out of my mind. Then when I saw you again the next morning, I knew that I had to have you." He informed her as he leaned against the headboard of the bed, lifting his arm up, for Haley to lay her head on his chest.

"You are the first woman that I could picture sharing the rest of my life with."

"No. You don't say." She said with mock disbelief as she giggled.

"I do say Mrs. Tyson." Haley tilted her head, her smile widen as she seen that sexy grin curving his mouth.

"Well, Mr. Tyson. Like the saying goes, be careful what you wish for. It just might come true."

# Epilogue

A year and a half later . . . .

"Honey? Where are the diapers?" Brad's panicked voice had Haley stifling a giggle as she waddled her way down the hallway. She smiled contently as she stood in the doorway, and seen her husband franticly searching for diapers. Things were finally looking up for the Tyson household. The police had finally tracked Adam down when he fled the state the night they questioned his whereabouts when their house was vandalized. He was picked up in Wisconsin when police pulled him over for speeding. Once the license plate number to dispatch, the police there learned there was a bench warrant issued for his arrest and was extradited back to Minnesota.

Adam gave a phony alibi before he left town. The police found his fingerprints on the rubber band that was wrapped around the brick. He was now in jail, awaiting his trial.

Megan was overjoyed now that she officially carried her Daddy's last name. Haley knew without a doubt that Brad loved both the girls, but she also knew there was a very special bond between Brad and Megan.

"There right there." Haley pointed a finger towards the bottom shelf of the changing table as her grin widened as she stepped inside the nursery.

"Carly's diaper just exploded on me again." Brad informed her. "Good god! What are we feeding this kid?" Brad asked as he fanned his hand in front of his face, waving off the offensive smell before he pulled the tabs to remove the unpleasant diaper.

"It's the transition from baby food, to big girl food." Haley explained as she neared the changing table with a fresh set of pajamas.

"Please tell me the doctor saw boy parts at your appointment today." Brad's pleading tone made her smile as he gestured towards her swollen belly. "Daddy's starting to feel outnumbered here." He playfully told Carly, making her giggle that adorable baby giggle.

"Well?" Haley drew out uncertainly as she squinted her eyes.

"What?" Brad erupted incredulously, causing Carly to giggle again.

"Looks like daddy's still going to be outnumbered." Brad playfully informed his little girl that was trying to pull the shirt Brad just placed over her head off.

"What do you think of that, Carly?" Brad looked down at Carly after he picked her up from the table and rested her on his hip. "You're going to have another sister to play with." Brad informed the bright eyed little girl that had drool running down her chin, as he placed his hand on Haley stomach and rubbed.

"Do you realize, I'm going to have to keep guys like myself away from my three little girls."

"Well." Haley drew out again, as an impish smile curved her mouth.

Brad quickly lifted his attention to Haley as he cocked his head to the side. "What do you mean, well?" He asked cautiously.

Haley didn't think she'd ever forget Brad's wide eyed, perplexed expression.

Haley slowly lifted her hand up and splayed her fingers, indicating four.

"What?" Brad's bemused features made her giggle.

"Where having twins?" He asked in an anxious tone.

When Haley coyishly nodded her head answering Brad question, his mouth dropped open as a smile of joy colliding with disbelief curved his stunned mouth.

He only hesitated for a few moments before he wrapped his one arm around Haley and squeezed her tight. "Honey, this is great!" His elated tone made Haley's grin even wider, as he placed a kiss on top of her head.

"You know what this means thought?" Brad asked a few moments later in a serious tone as he pulled away from her, just enough to look into her eyes.

"What?" Haley asked as she looked up at him, her eyebrows drawling together in confusion.

"Now where going to have to worry about all the D's."

Haley's eyes squinted as she continued to look up at him. "Huh?"

"You know. It rhymes with sticks." Brad said slowly, hoping she'd catch on.

When she shook her head indicating that she wasn't following. He rolled his eyes before leaning towards her ear and whispered.

"Where did you ever hear that?" Haley asked as she looked up at him again with a perplexed expression on her face.

"From a very smart man." He stressed

*~The End!~*